# Death is Delayed

**Outside the Circle Mystery, Volume 7**

Shereen Vedam

Published by Shereen Vedam, 2024.

DEATH IS DELAYED

**First edition. November 19, 2024.**

Copyright © 2024 Shereen Vedam.

ISBN: 978-1989036211

Written by Shereen Vedam.

*This book is dedicated to Mary Anning for demonstrating how to believe in myself.*

# Chapter One

Abbie's mother, Margaret Grimshaw, turned sixty-two last week. Not that Abbie could say a word about it.

For as long as she could remember, while her mother made a fuss about each of her four kids' birthdays, she refused to celebrate hers. So, Abbie and her three older brothers found other excuses to spend time with their mother around that "don't mention" date.

The ambulance services where she worked had called at mid-morning to say they'd hired an extra crew member, which unexpectedly freed Abbie up for the rest of the day. She'd texted her mother to see if they could meet up.

Her mother had jumped at the chance of a get-together and came over within the hour.

Margaret Grimshaw put away her coat and followed Abbie into her cottage's sitting room. "I thought we'd never find time for a quiet chat." She admired the coffee table where Abbie had readied tea and homemade custard cream biscuits. "This looks cozy, love."

Beside that tray sat a vase of fresh-cut yellow tulips and blush-pink peonies from the early summer garden.

"No one's expected home until this afternoon." Abbie plunked down on the sofa and patted the seat beside her. "Not even Robert."

"Where is the ghostly earl?" Her mother sank onto the sofa with a contented sigh. "Isn't his spirit tied to you?"

"Nica asked him to accompany her to school. She wanted help with a troublesome boy who's been pestering her."

"Ah, that makes sense. Robert is as fond of those children as he is of you. He will come up with a diplomatic way for Nica to deal with the matter."

"Yes," Abbie chuckled. "He is the epitome of a tactful Regency officer and gentleman–being both firm and kind. *And* since Jimi's also in school, this means we have all morning to catch up. How have you been, Mum?"

"Busy. I thought life would slow down after we turned 60. Yet, your father and I seem busier than ever at the pub. But I've taken the night off. I'm looking forward to spoiling the kids." Her mother's eyebrow rose. "You do still need a sitter?"

That would be her mother's indirect way of asking if Abbie's date tonight was on. Margaret Grimshaw rarely approached conversations directly.

"Yes. Callum and I are going to the theater."

Her mother nodded and leaned back, holding Abbie's gaze. "His heart is in the game, Abbie."

She gave her mother a quizzical glance. So was hers. "Your point?"

Margaret's gaze wandered away. "When your father doesn't think I'm looking, he has a certain look whenever he glances at one of my photos or reviews a video he's taken of me." She flashed her a smug smile. "As if he's found treasure. Callum has that same expression when he glances at you."

An old-fashioned way of looking at a relationship, but Abbie liked it. She'd been craving Callum's attention since the first time they met. Lately, her attraction to him had grown so strong that she often dreamt of them being a couple. She couldn't resist teasing, though. "If anyone has that look, Mum, it's me."

"No." Her mother's answer was firm.

Abbie started. Did her love for Callum not show on her face? Some days, the power of her feelings for the DCI overwhelmed her. "What do you mean?"

Her mother smoothed her summer dress, as if searching for the right words. "You remind me of a child who knows there's salted caramel ice cream in the freezer, but is afraid to get her hand slapped if she tries to sneak some before supper."

"Mum, I'm an adult! I eat ice cream anytime I want."

"Then why do you avoid reaching for it now?"

Considering her perilous Grimm work, Abbie and Callum had agreed to go slow.

"We can't move forward until Figg's previous, treacherous master is neutralized."

Figg was a huge part of Callum's life.

The *Roman*, her enemy, was most likely monitoring Abbie's movements. So, whenever she and Callum went out for a walk, they left Figg behind. Prying eyes would never catch the three of them together. It was dangerous enough for Callum to be seen in her company.

"Letting fear rule you is no way to live." Her mother's tone was unusually direct and cutting.

It was also unnerving, her mother leveling that argument at her. It had always been her precept for her kids.

Abbie reached for the plate of biscuits to give herself time to consider the uncomfortable truth behind her mother's words when a loud *whomp* shook the cottage. They glanced at each other.

"That came from the kitchen." Margaret jumped up.

"Arthur, shields up over me and Mum." The ring's power

sprang up as she raced after her mother.

Margaret stopped halfway to the kitchen. Abbie passed her and then swung back. Her mother was a Grimm, and her instincts were as accurate as Abbie's. "What's wrong?"

"This involves family." She met Abbie's gaze, brows knit, eyes narrowed. "I can't tell who it is, though."

"Let's find out." Abbie burst into the kitchen, shooting her Grimm cord out of her forefinger. At sighting a young woman standing on the other side of her kitchen table, she skidded to a halt, her breath stuck in her throat.

The newcomer in Abbie's kitchen wore a floor-length corseted gown with a high square neckline. Her charred dress smoked in parts. Her strawberry blond hair was braided, swept up at the back, and coiled to ride high on her head. Overtop it, her lace cap looked askew and her powdered cheeks had scorch marks.

"Ruby?" How could her gran be here? Abbie's mother had grown up an orphan because her father had died long before her birth and Ruby died shortly after Margaret was born.

"You're alive?" Margaret came around to Abbie's side.

"Or are you a ghost?" Ruby didn't seem older than when Abbie met her in 1959 during a time travel journey. Her gran had been twenty-seven then, and pregnant.

Ruby set an hourglass on the kitchen table, its white sand still dripping.

Not a ghost. Her grandmother had stolen that time travel artifact right out of Abbie's grip.

"Clearly, I'm alive, though barely." She sounded out of breath from whatever adventure she'd escaped. Ruby's gaze swerved to her daughter and settled, softening. "Hello, my dear. Lovely to see you again. How you've grown."

"If you're not dead, where have you been?" Her mother's tone dropped low and soft, filled with unspoken wishes.

*Why didn't you come when I was a child? When I needed someone to love me? To watch my back.*

"I was busy searching for the killer targeting Grimms," Ruby spoke in a brisk tone, her gaze skimming across everything in the kitchen except for her daughter. "You turned out fine, though, didn't you?" She gave a careless shrug as she studied the well-worn cupboards.

Ruby's wandering gaze finally returned to Margaret, but her lips twisted in disapproval as she skimmed over her daughter's generous hips. "Appears that you've let go of your training. Dangerous move for a Grimm."

Her mother's face turned red, her eyes flashing with ire.

Her throat tight with acrimony, Abbie put her arm around Margaret's shoulders, but her mother twisted free.

"Why are you here?" Margaret raised her head, her lips pinched. "Don't answer that. I don't care why you've come. It's too late." She gave a careless wave of her hand. "Turn over that hourglass and return to wherever you've been holed up in for the last sixty-two years."

Waves of loneliness flowed from her mother. This was why Margaret hated her birthdays. Because another year had passed without her mother. Abbie's heart wrung.

"Is that any way to greet me?" Ruby's clipped words suggested her mood, too, had soured. "Shows a sad lack of proper upbringing."

Abbie shook her head in warning. "Enough! Why are you here, Ruby? What's wrong?"

"Now that's how you greet a long-missed relative." Ruby smiled at Abbie, nodding her head as if in approval. "I need your help to kill someone."

"What's with that costume?" Margaret waved a hand at Ruby. "Who do you want to kill? Queen Anne?"

"Close. It's a man from her time. I wounded him severely with one of my wish bombs, but he got away." She released a frustrated sigh, her narrowed gaze spearing Abbie's with resolve. "He's the villain who has been killing Grimms over the centuries. Since you showed me how to use this lovely little hourglass–" she fingered the artifact before tucking it into her bosom "–I decided to take him out before he came after you two. But he got away. I need your help to find and finish him."

"No!" Margaret's decisive tone left no room for argument. She grabbed Abbie's hand. "She's not going anywhere with you."

"Don't be tiresome, Peggy." Ruby's gaze speared her daughter, her tone dropping to a low growl. "I'm in a hurry."

"My name is Margaret!"

"Mum's right." Her mother's direct speech was more worrisome than her animosity. Where had the soft-spoken woman she knew gone?

Though she directed her words to Ruby, it was her mother whom Abbie hoped would hear her past her fury. "My kids will be home later. If I'm to leave, I'll have to find a nanny. We also need to discuss this development with the Standard Bearers."

"You're not considering her request?" Her mother's voice rose to a higher pitch, bordering on panic.

"Who are these Standard Bearers?" Ruby's tone said she questioned Abbie's sanity. "Why would you ask their permission? You're a Grimm. We answer to no one."

"That's rich." Margaret's grip on Abbie's hand tightened as if she planned to physically prevent her daughter from leaving with Ruby. "Since you're here looking for Abbie's help."

Abbie eased out of her mother's hot hold and pulled out her mobile. "You met one of them when we visited. Judith."

"The witch?"

Abbie had forgotten that Ruby disapproved of witches. Ignoring her, she thumbed an alert to her crew. *Emergency SB meeting. New case. Stat.*

Ruby turned to glance out the window at the back garden and, beyond that, at St. Michael's graveyard.

Her gran may not approve of Abbie's methods, but this news of their enemy had far-reaching repercussions. "We've been searching for this immortal, too. I call him the Roman because that's the image I received of him from his dog. Do you know the Roman's true identity?"

Arms crossed, her expression bleak, Ruby faced her. Studying the landscape hadn't improved her mood. "He's not an immortal. He's as human as you and I."

Abbie shook her head at that assertion. "The vision of him as a young man was during Roman times. And you say you met him in the Queen Anne period? How can that be if he's mortal?"

Unless he, too, had a means of traveling through time.

Ruby held her gaze with confidence. "He's a mage who used a spell to prolong his life."

"Sounds as if we have much to discuss." Abbie turned to her mother. "There is tea and biscuits in the sitting room. Shall we adjourn there?"

Margaret released a heavy sigh, sounding defeated.

"If we're not leaving right away," Ruby gestured to herself, "I'd like to change first. It's hot in so many layers."

Abbie nodded and gauged her size. Ruby was a little shorter, but had more pronounced curves. "I have some freshly laundered clothing upstairs you can try on."

"Don't leave her alone with your artifacts." Margaret's warning earned her a glare from Ruby. "I'll wait for you in the sitting room. I need to let your father know I'll be late."

"Not on my account." Ruby gave a dismissive wave, the way Margaret had earlier. "Don't let us hold you up."

"Mum, please put on a fresh kettle and set out six more cups for us?"

Her mother glowered, but then nodded. She stood aside as they left the kitchen.

The only loo in the house was downstairs, so Abbie stopped there for Ruby to wash up before they headed upstairs.

Once in Abbie's bedroom, she gave her gran a pair of jeans and a T-shirt to try on for size.

"I guess Peggy... um... Margaret is upset with me." Ruby's tone was impassive, but her hands trembled as she undressed, suggesting something deeply troubled her.

"Since you weren't around, her uncle brought her up." Abbie tiptoed through this discussion as if she were navigating a minefield. "Your husband's brother. He was unkind. He trained her to be a killer."

"I know."

Abbie glanced at this twenty-something woman. It was hard to think of her as her gran. "How do you know what Mum went through?"

Ruby shed her gown and then had Abbie loosen her stays. Once that was off, she removed her scuffed, muddy shoes, torn stockings, and silk ribbon garters. She then dressed in Abbie's clothes, which were a little snug. All done in absolute silence.

Her gran tucked the hourglass back into her cleavage and tossed the wish bomb onto the bed. Abbie cringed, but it didn't explode. Both this wish bomb and that hourglass were their family artifacts. So, Ruby had a right to it. Abbie simply disapproved of how carelessly Ruby handled this one.

With a heavy sigh, her gran paced the room, glancing out the window. "This wasn't my first trip with the hourglass. I dropped in a few times to find out how my child made out in my absence. I was there for her graduation, marriage, and the birth of each of her children."

Abbie had only ever used her hourglasses once, afraid of how she might alter history if anything she did in the past affected their timeline. It sounded as if Ruby had used hers indiscriminately.

Ruby had not only used it often and with aplomb, but even traveled into the future. Why hadn't their timeline changed? Or had it, and she was unaware of how much?

Her gran's gaze was drenched in sorrow when she met Abbie's. "I was also there when your friends died." She took Abbie's hands and squeezed. "You took quite a hit."

"Why did you never contact Mum?"

"If I had," Ruby wrapped her arms around herself, "I would have never left her again and I had a killer to find."

Ruby's mood shifted like quicksilver, her eyes lighting up. "I saw a *Dr. Who* show on my first trip. Intriguing. Also, do you know there's a scientific theory that suggests no matter what we change in the past, the future will always end up the same?"

"Goddess Kali believes that in traveling through time," Abbie held Ruby's gaze, hoping her warning would get through, "we risk altering karma. That's why I didn't warn you that someone would try to kill you when I visited the past. Kali warned me to be careful. I'm sorry."

"Don't be." Ruby's smile turned cheeky, and she winked. "The report of my death was an exaggeration."

Abbie recognized the Mark Twain quote.

"Mainly spread by me." Ruby's words were unrepentant. "How else could I have gained the freedom to go after our enemy?"

"Who is he?" Should have been Abbie's first question.

Ruby shrugged, shaking her head. "He changes his name and identity as often as I do clothes. I finally caught up with him in 1703 in France and dealt a severe blow. Unfortunately, he deflected much of my wish bomb's blast, sending that force into the Bay of Biscay, which set off a cyclone."

Her gaze filled with chagrin, Ruby shrugged, as if she'd lost a pair of earrings instead of causing hundreds of deaths.

Abbie recalled reading about that cyclone in the early 1700s. Many ships had been lost. Folks had been devastated by flooding from France to the south of England. She gulped, her heart hammering, and sweat forming on her forehead. Did Ruby lack a conscience?

Color spread across Ruby's cheeks as if Abbie's reaction to her news finally registered. "It was a royal mess."

"One you caused!" Abbie's legs gave way, and she slumped into a chair, holding her hands to her chest. Had Ruby truly been responsible for that disaster, or would it have happened anyway? Abbie's gaze swerved to the wish bomb and she willed it back to her knapsack. "*And stay there!*"

Ruby's next words tumbled out, fast and intense. "In the confusion, I lost track of our villain. But he's wounded, Abbie. If we time our next trip to before that incident, together, we could prevent this disaster *and* take him out!"

"No! We're not changing major past events." Abbie was resolved on this point. "Who knows what consequences there might be? We can't calculate what other damage we might do by altering what is now history."

Ruby flopped onto her back on the bed and spoke to the ceiling. "What do you propose?"

Abbie laid out her red line. "If we go, we will not be bringing any wish bombs."

"What?" The word came out of Ruby in a squeak. Her hands spread out as she groped for the wish bomb and came up empty-handed. She sat up, arms and legs crossed. "You took it! How else are we to finish him?"

"We will work with what we find in that time period. Those are my terms."

Ruby's lips pinched, as if she wanted to argue with Abbie's stipulation, demand she return the wish bomb. Then her gran's shoulders dropped. "I don't believe I'm meant to kill him, anyway." Her tone turned gruff. "You are. During your visit to my time, only the artifacts you touched came alive. Those are the ones that come when I call. It was as if you'd awoken a new ability in them to hear me from a distance."

Ruby sounded so peeved that she couldn't wake her other artifacts that a defiant corner of Abbie purred.

Her gran raised her arms. "Alright, we do it your way."

The tension in Abbie's shoulders eased. That decision could have gone the wrong way. Ruby's forceful personality had a way of steamrolling over others' views.

The doorbell rang. "That'll be the Standard Bearers gathering." Abbie stood and held out her hand. "Come on. I'll introduce you."

Abbie and Ruby entered the sitting room to find Yousef seated in a chair beside Margaret. He was dressed in a smart suit.

The cat-shifter stood and sent the newcomer a thorough once-over. After introductions, he shook her hand. "Welcome to Chipstead, Mrs.?"

"It's the tradition for our family members to keep the Grimshaw name." Abbie's mother's tone was cool, her glance icy enough to freeze. "Unless you've parted from that formality, too, along with mothering your child?"

"Call me Ruby." Abbie's gran kept her attention entirely on Yousef, her admiring glance skimming over him from round black spectacles to pointed polished shoes. Ignoring Margaret, she sat beside him.

Yousef met Abbie's gaze, no doubt picking up on the animosity between the two women. Trapped between Margaret and Ruby, was that a hint of desperation in his eyes?

The doorbell rang again, giving Abbie the excuse to bolt to check on her next guest.

She shoved aside her guilt at abandoning Yousef. He was a grown man. He could handle Ruby and her mother for a few minutes.

# Chapter Two

It was Talin and Judith on Abbie's doorstep. Behind them, in St. Michael's car park, her kids raced home with Robert. That completed their group.

Back in the sitting room, Abbie made introductions.

"Do we call them both gran?" Nica's frowning glance went from Margaret to Ruby.

"You could try Gran Ruby and Gran Margaret." Judith's suggestion fell flat with both kids, who crossed their arms and shook their heads.

"I know." Jimi turned to Ruby. "We'll call you Nana. That's what River calls his gran."

Ruby shook her head. "That makes me sound like a nanny goat."

Margaret smiled at the boy. "I'd love that moniker."

"Glad that's settled." Abbie then summarized why Ruby had descended on her kitchen. "She wants us to return to when the Roman was injured and finish him while he's weak."

"Oh, no!" Nica ran over to Abbie's side, wrapping her arms around her. "You almost didn't return the last time you time traveled." She leaned back to catch her eye. "What if something goes wrong again, like another cyclone?"

Abbie cuddled Nica and kissed her forehead. "My instinct tells me I'm meant to go, Nica. But I'm unsure what we should take with us." She turned to her group. "Certainly nothing destructive, to ensure we don't alter the past."

A discussion erupted then, as that statement suggested Abbie intended to accompany Ruby. Everyone offered their opinions on this plan.

All except for Margaret Grimshaw. She was in her chair, arms folded, lips pressed, and her cheeks flushed.

Abbie allowed the lively and contentious talk between her Standard Bearer crew and Ruby to carry on without interruption. What worried her more was her mother's silence.

Normally, her mother would either have left the room, wanting nothing to do with Abbie's Grimm activities, or suggest something innocuous that would nudge Abbie toward exactly what her mother wanted her to do. She wasn't even snapping at Ruby as she had done earlier.

Her mother had great instincts for her daughter's welfare, similar to Abbie's Grimm instinct to know when something she planned was right or wrong. Her mother's lack of reaction, therefore, concerned her. What was going on inside Margaret Grimshaw's head?

"You're not going alone with her." Her mother's bleak voice broke in, proving Abbie's instincts correct. That categorical declaration, so unlike her mother's veiled suggestions, silenced everyone.

"Mum–"

"During our Diwali celebration in Abbie's garden," Judith's soft, but firm voice broke into Abbie's pleading tone, "we all received the impression from Kali that none of the SB crew were invited to join Abbie on her upcoming journey."

"If none of you will protect Abbie from that one," Margaret's head tilted toward Ruby, "I will."

Ruby released a bark of laughter that earned her daughter's glower. "Sorry, Peggy, but you relinquished your Grimm role decades ago. Now you're well past sixty, even if you're not in the throes of your feminine change time, you're in no fit shape to retake your Grimm duties. I'm shocked you're still alive. Our kind rarely survives into our fifties, never mind beyond that."

"Ruby!" Abbie cringed for her mother. And that last comment about Grimms dying young was news to her.

Nica shook within Abbie's hold. Jimi moved closer to his sister, patting her shoulder, his eyes wide and worried.

Abbie gave Ruby a head shake.

Focused on her daughter, her gran ignored that warning. "You'd be a hindrance, not a help, if you insist on trailing us."

"You sound like your brother-in-law." Considering how much Margaret had hated her uncle, that said a lot. "If you hoped that attempt at intimidation would cow me, you don't know me at all. But then how could you, since you were never a mother to me? Understand this: if Abbie goes on this mission, you'll both have to put up with me."

Ruby's face flushed pink at that rebuke and she turned to Abbie, raising an imperious eyebrow, as if she expected Abbie to slay that ultimatum.

Nica ran over to Margaret. "I want Nana to go."

By the besotted look on her mother's face, Margaret Grimshaw couldn't have asked for a better birthday present than Nica's passionate support.

"I'm a Standard Bearer!" Nica's tone was proud as she held her head up high. "So, I have a say in our decisions. I'll only agree to Abbie leaving if Nana goes along."

"Me, too." Jimi ran over to Margaret's other side, making his allegiance clear. Though he was growing up, his support of his sister never wavered, something that thrilled Abbie. These two would look out for each other if anything tragic ever happened to her.

Judith stood and strolled over to take her stand behind Margaret's chair. "Granny Chan used to tell me tales of your mother's exploits when she was a working Grimm. In our absence, there's no one shrewder you could take with you."

Robert limped over to stand beside Judith, meeting Abbie's gaze with a firm stare. "Your mother has great Grimm instincts. I would prefer if she were with you to offer sound guidance. Especially if plans change en route, as they did on your last time travel adventure."

Yousef joined the other SB crew, adding his support. "No offense meant, but Ruby is an unknown quantity, while your mother is a well-known and tested Grimm with whom I have complete faith and trust."

Talin was the last to rise to his feet. He ambled over to Margaret, knelt beside her, and took her hand.

Her mother's eyes widened, and she leaned back.

"A little energy boost can't hurt." The electromagnetic wizard gave her a friendly smile. "May I?"

Margaret gave him a bemused glance and nodded.

Abbie sensed the waves of energy flowing into her mother from Talin.

"That should level the playing field." Talin swiveled to address Abbie. "The others are correct. She'll be an asset. I'm in favor of her going along."

"Thank you." Margaret gave everyone surrounding her a grateful glance.

Ruby crossed her arms. "Abbie, you're not seriously going to allow these people to dictate what we do, are you?"

Abbie couldn't stop her lips from tilting upward. "We're

the Standard Bearers. We work together, not against each other. If they think this is the best way forward for us, that's exactly what we will do."

Ruby's cheeks flushed darker, but she stayed silent.

"Yay!" Nica and Jimi ran back to hug Abbie.

"Now that's settled," Robert's gaze turned grave, "you should reconsider your decision on not taking any artifacts with you, Miss Grimshaw."

This was Robert's usual MO. "What do you suggest?"

"You have your cord and ring, but all three of you should take one further artifact each that might help you during your upcoming travels." At Ruby's raised-armed *whoop* of cheer, he sent her a disapproving frown. "Not a weapon, but a helpful tool. The year 1703 is far different from this time. You will need specialized assistance."

Abbie nodded.

"Shall I fetch your rucksack?" Nica jumped up.

"No need." Abbie moved the tea tray aside, focused on her artifacts, and then tapped the empty coffee table. "Come here."

Items landed on the wooden surface in a clatter, all except for the bag of wish bombs.

"Impressive!" Ruby studied her choices.

Her artifacts' instant response pleased Abbie, too. It was good to test her connection to them now and then and have it confirmed.

Her mother was also inspecting the scattered items, sifting through them with her forefinger. "I'd forgotten how many we have. How do we know which one to take?"

"Who needs to go with Mum?"

Items moved aside to allow a thimble to slide out from

their midst and speed toward Margaret.

"I've never used this one." Her mother picked up the thimble, her brows wrinkling and eyes crinkling as she studied it. "Doesn't it have something to do with clothing?"

"Ask its name and what it does." Abbie sat back.

Margaret held up the thimble. "Who are you?"

*"Marie-Jeanne."* The thimble had a strong French accent within Abbie's head. *"Bonjour, Madam Margaret."*

Her mother chuckled while her SB crew started. Abbie's Grimm cord must have broadcast the thimble's response to all those present.

It was her mother's reaction that caught and held Abbie's attention. This was the first light emotion her mother had displayed since Ruby's arrival. It enlivened her face.

Ruby's gaze was transfixed on her daughter, too.

*"J'aide à changer de vêtements."* Abbie's cord translated. *"I help change clothes."*

"Perfect." Yousef slapped his hand on his armrest. "Since you won't have Judith along to assist with era-appropriate clothing."

"My turn." Ruby leaned forward in her chair and pushed the artifacts back to make room on the table directly ahead of her. "Who's coming with me?"

Artifacts tumbled over each other before a small, round, ribbed orange item with a short thick stem slid forward.

"It's a pumpkin!" Nica giggled, her face lighting up with delight. "Like in Cinderella, can it become a carriage?"

At Ruby's inquiry, the item introduced himself as Basil. *"I can transform into any vehicle you require."*

"Love it." Ruby pocketed the artifact. "Wish I'd thought to

take him on my earlier travels."

"Travels? Plural?" Margaret speared Ruby with a suspicious frown. "How often have you used the hourglasses?"

Ruby winked at her. "If you prove me wrong and help us make it back alive, I might tell you."

Margaret's face flushed before she glanced at Abbie, pointedly ignoring her cheeky mother. "Your turn."

The doorbell rang.

"Expecting anyone else, Abbie?" Yousef asked.

She shook her head and stood.

Robert strode to the front window. "It's DCI Radford."

"I'll be right back." Abbie hurried to the front door. If she was to go on this trip with Ruby, he needed to know she wouldn't make their date tonight.

She opened the door, and on seeing Callum's craggy features, and getting trapped in his dark gray gaze, her heart skipped a beat, while a blush heated her face. She'd been obsessing about their date tonight until Ruby showed up and shoved her romantic plans clean out of her mind.

Figg licked her hand.

Abbie's heart warmed at the sight of the black and white dog, whose forlorn gaze could ensnare her as effectively as his master.

Except, while Callum might be a welcome sight, Figg was not. She scanned the horizon for anyone who might have noticed the three of them here together. Her garden was lush with spring flowers, but empty of prying eyes.

"What is he doing here with you?" She pointed to the dog, who leaned against her jean-clad legs in search of a pet. "Get inside before someone sees you two." She rushed both into her home and shut the door.

"I'm unsure what I'm doing here." Callum's gaze rested on her lips a moment before sweeping up to meet hers. "One moment we were out for our walk by a lake and the next, we were outside your picket gate."

"Figg brought you?" He'd transported Callum using magic before, but only to avoid danger.

"I didn't ask him to. Why would I, when we're set to meet later?" He glanced around the empty entryway. "By the look of the number of vehicles in your car park, seems like you're having a party. Do we need to cancel tonight?"

"Yes." Sincere regret swamped her, leaving her cold, a little lonely, and a whole lot frustrated. "We're holding an emergency Standard Bearers' meeting. My grandmother Ruby arrived unexpectedly and wants me to return to 1703 and deal Figg's old master a fatal blow while he's wounded."

"Right...1703?" He glanced at Figg. "What about him? Will he and I still find each other if you take out his master back then?" Callum's words were loaded with concern. "Are you sure you need to go? Sounds dangerous."

Abbie squeezed his cool fingers. "I won't be going alone. Grimm women are uniting for this trip. And I'm not doing this to hurt Figg."

"I know you love him as much as I do." His still worried gaze met hers.

"Callum, we won't ever be free to move forward until Figg's master is no longer a threat."

He stroked Figg's forehead, and the dog leaned into the pet, whining in pleasure. "What happens to those Figg killed in the past? Like that farmer's son at the fair, where you first met the dog? Will your trip affect how that case turned out?"

That's how she'd first learned about the Roman. She hadn't considered that angle. His comments always made her see a situation in a new light. She tilted her head toward her sitting room. "We haven't finished our discussion yet. I'll bring up how what we plan might affect what happened in the past."

Callum nodded and then fished in his pocket. He brought out a handkerchief-wrapped article. When he unwrapped it, inside was Levi, her compass artifact. It was excellent at locating people. She'd lent it to him to help him with his police work. He tucked Levi into her palm. "Would you take this? To find your way back to me?"

Lost for words, she glanced at Levi. The metal was still warm from being close to Callum's skin. What if Figg wasn't the only one she lost because of this journey? Would she even be a Grimm on her return if that bus in London had never blown up? Would she have ever met Callum? An acute pain stabbed her chest at that loss. She pulled him closer.

His arms enfolded her and their lips met. Abbie wove her arms around his neck, not wanting to let go. She breathed in his blend of cedar and sandalwood, imprinting him as much as he'd seemed to claim her.

When she drew back, her lips tingled from his touch, while her heart ached at the possibility of returning to a life without Callum. He, too, appeared white as a sheet, as if he were devastated by where his thoughts had led him.

Bending, Abbie hugged Figg, heartsore about how her journey might affect the dog, too.

When she rose to her feet, her emotions under better control, it was to face a Callum who also seemed to have regained his aplomb. He brushed her cheek with a finger. "See you soon, *ya daft wee shite.*"

Abbie was still chuckling long after he and Figg had walked away, waiting for his Rover's tail lights to drive out of sight. Only then did she shut her door and return to the sitting room. She held up Levi for all to see. "I'll be taking this."

Robert nodded. "Good choice. It can help you track our villain."

Ruby shook her head. "I've never been able to get that to work."

"Talin tied the compass to the metal cladding on St. Michael's spire to get Levi to triangulate." Abbie turned to her electromagnetic wizard friend. "Will that work in the past?"

"I have an idea about how to do that." Talin hurried over to the front window overlooking the church, and his hands moved energy lines. He returned to his chair, flashing her a self-satisfied smirk. "I've energized the spire, reaching back into its past, to when the church was first built."

"I didn't know you could do that." Judith glanced at him with respect.

"I've been studying cellular memory." Talin shrugged. "Works for atoms, too. The memory thread leads to different places and even different times. Though I've never followed that thread so far before. Shocking, but I'm sure it worked."

"Can the compass reach this church from France?" Ruby sounded skeptical.

*"I can reach any point as long as it is on Earth."* Levi sounded confident.

"Great." Abbie glanced at her SB crew. "I have another concern we should discuss. If we take out our enemy in the past, that will most likely affect Figg, too. Callum wondered if that dog would still be around when we returned. Or the farmer's son, whom Figg killed at his master's behest? The Roman and Figg have slain many people. Aside from any karmic effects, how might that transform our present?"

"Isn't that the point?" Ruby shrugged, as if these worries didn't faze her. "Don't we want to prevent those deaths?"

Abbie fingered Levi's cool metal surface engraved with odd symbols, her thoughts roiling. She didn't want to return home to discover Callum had married someone else, or that Figg was no longer in their lives.

Ruby rapped on the coffee table to catch Abbie's attention. "Whatever happens because we've taken out our enemy has to be for the better. Think of those you lost in London. They might still be alive when we return."

"As painful as the bombing incident was," Abbie held Ruby's gaze, clutching the compass until its edges bit into her palm, "I've come to terms with it. If not for that incident, I might never have come into my talent. Or formed the Standard Bearers."

Abbie tucked away the compass in her back pocket before cuddling her kids closer. "If not for those events, Nica and Jimi might not be in my life. Taking all that into consideration, I'm unsure what we plan is the right course."

Ruby's brooding gaze wandered around the silent room, and then she jumped to her feet. "Life might be different." She strode between the sofa and the coffee table toward Abbie. "It might end up better."

"Look out!" Robert shouted. "She has the hourglass."

Not only had Ruby taken out the hourglass, but she'd

turned it over.

Ruby's hand clamped over Abbie's forearm.

"No!" Margaret shouted as the time portal opened up behind Ruby, directly over her chair.

Before Abbie could draw breath, the time portal sucked her and Ruby into it.

Margaret jumped up and grabbed Abbie's leg.

The portal began to close and Abbie pulled her mother inside the tunnel before it cut her in two.

Yousef reached into Abbie's artifacts on the coffee table and held up the other hourglass, the one with pink sand that acted as the beacon that would call them home before the last sand particle fell. In the deafening *whoosh* of the portal, he pointed toward her and then held up two fingers and then four.

Good reminder. She had twenty-four hours to return home or risk being stuck wherever and whenever they landed.

The last sight Abbie had was of Robert rushing toward the small opening remaining of the portal door. It slammed shut before he reached it. He had spoken, though, pointing inside the tunnel, but all she'd heard in the din of the portal door closing was one word. "Lizzy."

Abbie, Margaret, and Ruby turned around to the new opening that had formed behind them. Abbie's thoughts, though, lingered with Robert. Why had he mentioned his daughter's name? Lizzy died in 1816, and shortly after, the authorities hanged him.

The tunnel shuddered, and then the opening that had been drawing them forward, shut. Instantly, another opening formed. This new door pulled them in a divergent direction.

"What's happening?" Her mother's shouted question was

steeped with unease.

"I don't know." Ruby also sounded concerned. "This has never happened to me. See what you've done by inserting yourself into our journey."

"Are you blaming me?" Her mother slapped a hand on her chest.

"We're still moving." Abbie studied the new opening, hanging onto her mother. "What matters is that we're headed somewhere." She sent up a prayer that this new destination would take them back home to St. Michael's.

The portal shuddered again, and then Abbie, her mother, and Ruby were shoved toward the latest opening.

"Arthur, raise shields over me and my family. Use their artifacts as your touchpoint."

She'd barely finished speaking before all three of them fell out of the portal and toward the ground. They rolled down a grassy slope, tumbling over each other.

*Ouch. Ow. Oof.*

# Chapter Three

Once they rolled to a stop on the grassy ground, Ruby, flattened by her daughter, shoved Margaret aside so she could stand. "I'm never taking you two traveling again. When I'm alone, my landings are graceful."

"We're not supposed to be with you now." Margaret sounded as incensed as Ruby. She rose to her feet, brushing herself down. "What kind of mess have you landed us in?"

Abbie stood as well, noting she wasn't injured, and neither were her two companions. "*Thank you, Arthur.*"

Her ring buzzed her left forefinger. She breathed a sigh of relief at that confirmation. If Arthur was active, this meant the other artifacts with them should work, too. "We need to figure out where and when we've arrived."

"It should be 1703." Ruby's movements were frantic as she glanced around. "We're inland, whereas I pictured arriving on the coast. At least these trees should hide us until we're ready to show ourselves to the public."

"Over there." Margaret pointed behind Abbie. "Isn't that St. Michael's steeple? Except, it's not tipped. Must mean we're near where we left, but not in our time."

"We're not even in France?" Ruby's tone rose to a high pitch. "Alright." She swung around to glare at Margaret. "Which one of you was thinking about Kent while we were inside the time portal?"

Stomach knotted at what she might have inadvertently done, Abbie raised her hand. "That was me. Sorry, Ruby, but you took me by surprise. Then Robert pointed at us and shouted out his daughter's name. It made me think about that time. Lizzy died in 1816."

"Are you saying we might not even be in the right time?" Placing her hands on her head, Ruby groaned.

Her pulse pattering, Abbie glanced around. "Whenever this is, the clear blue sky, wildflowers in bloom, and this warm temperature suggests we've landed in early summer."

She didn't add that the authorities had arrested Robert in June 1816 for the murder of his daughter. The event she'd been thinking about when the time portal changed direction. Hard to believe the hourglass had tuned into her thoughts despite Ruby holding it.

The three of them were Grimms, all able to command these artifacts that had belonged to her family over generations. This reaction of the hourglass added a new nuance. It hinted that while all three of them could use their artifacts, her hold on them had primacy.

After she came into her power three years ago, the artifacts had come awake in her presence. A few had even traveled vast distances to reach her. What she hadn't realized was that her connection to her artifacts was stronger than any other Grimm's control.

Abbie shivered. This gave more credence to Ruby's belief that Abbie was the only one who could get rid of their enemy once and for all, that she was indeed the Grimm Guardian referred to by the prophecy.

From the treetops, the hoot of an owl sounded, silencing the tweets and chirps from nearby birds and insects. A scurrying in the underbrush suggested a small creature went into hiding.

"We should attempt to return home before we risk altering this timeline." Margaret held out her arm to Ruby. "Hand over the hourglass."

"Not in this lifetime or any other." Ruby tucked it deep into her cleavage.

"We have twenty-four hours to decide what to do." Abbie aimed for a calm tone. "If we don't turn over the hourglass to take us home by then, we'll be stuck wherever or whenever this is."

Since they were near St. Michel's, if they were indeed in Robert's time, could he be nearby? Possibly, but he wouldn't recognize her. Still, seeing Robert when he was alive was a tempting possibility. When would she ever get such a chance again? Never, that's when.

If this was June, he was married, with a child. No, by June 1816, Lizzy was dead. He and his wife, Pauline, would be in deep mourning.

Also, it was unsafe for her to talk to him. With a heavy sigh, she gave up that tempting possibility. The sooner they returned home, the better, before she changed this past.

"Could we attempt to re-open the portal and carry on to where we were supposed to go?" At Ruby's thoughtful tone, Margaret caught Abbie's gaze and shook her head vehemently.

"Neither Klaus nor the hourglasses ever mentioned if a secondary trip was possible." To allay Ruby's suspicions, Abbie spoke in a conversational tone. "But if you let me speak to the hourglass, I can ask it if that's possible."

"Nope." Ruby backed away. "Sorry, love. I don't trust either of you with this artifact."

At least that artifact hadn't broken as it had the last time

Abbie trim traveled.

Ruby held up the hourglass. "There is another way to find out if we can carry on with our journey. I can ask this."

"Wait!" Margaret cried out, clutching her temple.

"What's wrong?" Abbie hurried over to her mother.

"Someone's in trouble."

"Someone's always in trouble somewhere." Ruby rolled her eyes, her tone brusque. "Whoever it is, they're not our priority."

"This has to be family." Margaret glared at Ruby with pained eyes. "I only get these premonitions when someone related to us is in danger."

"Who could that possibly be?" Ruby asked in a skeptical tone.

"One of our ancestors?" Abbie glanced around with worry. They were in a copse of trees. With St. Michael's visible on the horizon and the sound of a stream nearby, surely a road couldn't be far off. "If a family member is in trouble, that means we've been brought here, at this time, to help."

Abbie firmly believed her Grimm missions were blessed. The resultant sparks that her Standard Bearers' fist bumps elicited were a symbol of divine intervention. Too bad they hadn't done one this time. "Where is this person located, Mum?"

Margaret pointed to their left and headed off through the underbrush with a determined stride. "We must hurry."

Abbie followed her mother while speaking to her gran over her shoulder. "If I'm the only one who can vanquish our enemy, Ruby, going to 1703 alone won't do you any good."

With a long-suffering huff, Ruby's footsteps trudged after them through the undergrowth.

"Get that hourglass away from her." Margaret's whispered words were full of venom. Her ferocity set Abbie aback. "She won't let me near her or I'd do it."

"Mum." Abbie softened her voice, "are you faking this premonition?"

"No. Someone is in trouble. A child. She feels as close to my heart as you or one of your brothers. This one is family."

"If we're staying and plan to interact with people," Ruby hurried to catch up, "we'll need to change clothes to suit this time." She gave Abbie and Margaret a side glance full of speculation, as if she didn't care for their whispering. "Jeans and T-shirts won't suit." She pointed to their feet. "Nor will trainers."

"I agree, but for now, jeans and trainers are more suitable for a wilderness trek." Abbie's mind stayed glued to her mother's last words. "Family in trouble could be why Kali warned me that none of my Standard Bearers should travel with me on my next journey. Only Mum's special senses would have recognized a Grimm family member in danger. She's meant to be here on this journey."

Ruby *harrumphed* at that, but kept pace from that point onward. Once they cleared the line of trees, a rough pitted dirt road came into view.

Thumping hoofs and clanking metal announced they were about to have company. They scurried behind bushes to avoid being seen in their modern attire.

Two horses strapped to a two-wheeled carriage trundled their way, with a woman expertly handling the reins. A young child sat beside her, reading from an open book on her lap.

Excitement sent Abbie's pulse sprinting at the sight of the

curricle and its occupants. She'd only ever seen a vehicle like that while it was stationary in a museum. Seeing it being driven was much cooler.

Abbie eyed the woman's dress. "That pretty empire-style gown, Spencer, and round, stylish bonnet confirms we've arrived in Regency times."

The young girl beside the woman wore a white dress of a similar style with a shawl over her shoulders.

"Mum, could that be the child you sensed?"

Margaret shook her head. "No. The one I'm drawn to is younger and terrified." As the carriage drove past them, her head tilted in the direction where the carriage had come from. "It's a young girl who is several miles down that road."

"Then, since time is of the essence, we'd better use a carriage." Ruby pulled out her tiny pumpkin artifact and strode toward the road. Abbie and Margaret followed her.

Ruby placed the pumpkin on the empty dirt road and stepped back. "We'll need a horse-drawn carriage, Basil." She ran a critical eye over Margaret's form, her gaze settling on her daughter's wide hips long enough to make her blush.

"A gig is out. We need a vehicle big enough to hold four in case we have to transport this child to someplace safe. It must also be swift enough to aid us in escaping trouble. A lightweight four-wheeled carriage should do. With a coachman, footman, and a postillion, plus four horses."

"How are we to find all those people and livestock?" Margaret gazed at Ruby, askance.

"Post-chaises don't drive or care for themselves." Ruby shook pinched fingers at Margaret. "It's not like being handed the key to a car, Peggy."

"Stop calling me that!"

"Then how would you like me to address you, dear?" Ruby gave Margaret a gentle smile that should have melted the hardest of hearts.

Lips tight, Margaret snapped her response. "May we hurry? Or we'll be too late to be of any help."

Ruby returned her attention to her pumpkin artifact. "Basil, can you arrange all that we need?"

"*Yes.*"

"Meanwhile, I'll fashion us appropriate clothing." Her mother extracted her thimble. "Marie-Jeanne, I need gowns from early 1816. Suitable for summer, including outerwear, hats, and half-boots. Make Abbie's white, mine dark green, and the one for—for Ruby in..."

"Brown for me, with a half pelisse. I prefer to blend into the background. Easier to remain unnoticed that way."

Abbie's gaze transfixed on Ruby. Her gran's jeans and T-shirt were replaced with a cream gown beneath a beautiful brown pelisse, half-boots, and a helmet-shaped bonnet that cupped her head. With her blond hair curling around her face beneath the cap, she looked breathtaking.

Margaret was soon draped in a pretty dark green pelisse that reached to her feet over a pale green traveling gown.

Abbie twirled to show off her white gown, with its short pink Spencer jacket, and matching boots. She adored Regency clothing. It was the best part of attending a re-enactment fair. That, and the dancing.

Ruby pointed toward the brush. "Here they come."

A crow flew out of the copse of trees. The bird swooped over Abbie's head, and she ducked. A flare warmed her as the crow landed beside a smart, four-wheeled open wooden carriage. The large vehicle sat where the tiny pumpkin had once rested on the road.

In a flash of light, the crow transformed into a blue-and-white liveried footman standing at attention.

With a rapid-fire *ki-ki-ki-ki*, a goshawk flew overhead and landed on the box seat at the front of the carriage and became the coachman, outfitted in smart livery that matched the footman.

A family of four red foxes gave high-pitched barks as they raced out of the woods to position themselves ahead of the carriage. The two kits moved ahead of their parents. In a flare, they changed into sturdy chestnut horses, flicking their tails and neighing.

The central wood shaft extending from the body of the carriage lifted. Leather straps attached the horses to the carriage. A sparrow landed on the lead horse at the front left and became the postillion who would guide them.

"Shall we go, ladies?" Ruby stepped up to the vehicle. "We have a child to find."

The footman opened the carriage door and folded down small wooden steps before holding out his hand to assist them.

Ruby pulled Margaret to sit beside her, forcing Abbie to sit facing the two women with her back to the front of the carriage. She didn't mind, for the upholstered seat was quite comfortable and left her plenty of room. This also gave her a good view of her mother and grandmother. They were unlike each other in stature, but both were Grimms with a determination that mirrored each other perfectly.

"How do I direct the carriage?" Her mother frowned,

gazing out the window. "I don't know where our quarry is located, exactly."

"If you think about where you wish to go, Mum, this carriage will head in that direction."

"Try not to contradict her instructions, Abbie." Ruby adjusted her hourglass down her cleavage. She gave her granddaughter a keen look that suggested she'd come to the same conclusion about how these artifacts reacted to Abbie's wishes. That explained why she wanted to sit beside Margaret rather than Abbie.

Distance from her artifacts wasn't a hindrance to Abbie's control of them. Ruby didn't need to know that just yet. She glanced out the window as the carriage rolled on, crunching bits of gravel that pinged off the underside.

There was little traffic on this road, but they passed a haywain and turned down several lanes. After a while, their carriage made a sharp turn into a narrow lane.

Margaret peered out the window. "We're close."

Since Abbie's view was on where they come from, it afforded little useful information. At her mother's warning, though, her Grimm instincts kicked in. Something significant, even life-changing, was about to happen.

"There's a carriage barreling toward us from up ahead." Ruby's warning was clipped. "The horses will crash into each other if we don't move aside, but there's no place to pull over."

Abbie looked out the window. The road ahead was empty. Was this Ruby's instinct coming into play? Margaret could sense family in trouble, and Abbie's Grimm senses showed her the right course to take. She'd wondered how Ruby's Grimm talent manifested. Hers must be foreshadowing.

The carriage stopped, and Ruby pushed open the side door and leapt out. Abbie grabbed her mother, and they went out the other side of the carriage. They hurried into the underbrush.

Their vehicle flared before turning back into a tiny pumpkin in the middle of the lane. All the birds and animals who'd staffed it scurried away. Around a bend ahead, a second carriage raced toward them. Its wheels drove past the pumpkin artifact without touching it.

As the carriage passed her, Abbie caught a clear glimpse of the inside. Figg stared back, maintaining eye contact. At the dead look in his gaze, she shivered. The dog was mindlessly following his master's orders, just as he had the first time Abbie met him after he'd killed a farmer.

Frozen in place, her arms covered in goosebumps, Abbie tore her gaze from Figg's bloody muzzle, and for one split second, glimpsed the dark outline of a man sitting across from the dog. He stared in the other direction, presenting her with the back of his head. All she gained was an impression of a tall, gray-haired gentleman.

The carriage continued without slowing. Even the coachman only stared straight ahead, never turning his head to acknowledge the women on the side of the road. If anything, the carriage might even have sped up.

Once that vehicle was lost to sight, Ruby rushed over to Abbie and Margaret. "I think that was our enemy."

Her mother's wide gaze was focused on the road ahead.

Watching her mother, Abbie worried that the state the dog had been in didn't bode well for the child they sought. "Mum, Figg was inside that carriage. His muzzle was bloody."

"The girl's still alive." Her mother ran up the road. "But she's in dire danger."

Ruby collected their pumpkin artifact and ran after Margaret.

Abbie followed them up the empty road, her gaze switching between her family ahead and the disappearing carriage at their rear. What if the Roman came after them?

Margaret raced on ahead. The energy assist Talin had given her must be spurring her steps.

Abbie caught up to Ruby. "You were right. That was the Roman, but what made you think that?"

"He seemed to recognize me." Instead of being terrified by that detection, Ruby sounded as if she had relished the fact. "His eyes practically bulged with shock. And he was with that dog of his, wasn't he?"

"Yes, that was Figg." The lane behind them remained empty. Why wasn't he chasing after them? Could it be because he *had* recognized Ruby? Was he still frightened of the woman who almost killed him? Even if so, she wouldn't put it past him to set a trap for them. "What if he sends Figg after us?"

"I doubt it." Ruby huffed, too, as they ran. "He seemed scared. I'm sure I weakened him enough at our last encounter that he won't readily confront me again or risk losing his dog."

"Unless he's recovered since that incident. You met him a hundred-plus years ago, Ruby."

"Do you two smell that?" Margaret paused up ahead. "Something's burning."

"A house." Ruby sounded confident of that.

Abbie and Ruby caught up to Margaret as they turned a corner and came across a large mansion in flames. "We're too late." Ruby came to a halt, catching her daughter's arm. "I sense several dead inside there."

"Not the one we seek." Margaret pulled away and raced toward the burning building. "She's alive. And terrified. We must save her before the flames reach her!"

It was hard to keep up with her mother's remarkable speed. Abbie finally caught up to her, barely a few feet from the burning house, and grabbed her around her body to halt her.

Ruby arrived to take a firm hold of Margaret's arm and together, they forcibly dragged her back from the fire.

Margaret struggled within their holds. "Let me go!"

Ruby sent Abbie a wary glance over her daughter's head as they restrained her from running into danger.

"She's inside, I tell you." Margaret wrestled to free herself.

"I believe you, Mum." Abbie coughed, the acrid smoke irritating her throat. "But we need to get her out without getting ourselves killed."

"Your ring's shield is over me. I can get inside without getting burned. She's family, Abbie!"

"I know, but if anyone goes inside that burning building, it should be me. I can extend my shield over the child to get her out safely."

That assurance finally got through to her mother, and she stopped struggling. "I sense she's below ground. Perhaps past the kitchen?"

"I'll use Levi to get her exact location." She loosened her hold on her mother. "You two stay here. Arthur's shield will stay over both of you, so you'll be safe if the Roman or Figg returns."

Ruby nodded, her grip on Margaret unyielding as her wary

gaze met Abbie's. "Be careful."

Waves of heat buffeted Abbie from the burning front doors. The entire house was aflame, fire billowing out of the roof and windows. She slapped at a stray spark that scorched her gown. Her fingers came away covered in ash, but, thanks to Arthur, she remained unharmed. She might need more protection inside the burning house.

"Arthur, can you adjust my shield so I can breathe clean air inside that house, along with not being burned or hit by falling debris?"

Her shield's vibration changed. *"Done."*

She moved in close to the flaming doors, pleased when she didn't feel the heat of the flames licking so close to her. Then Abbie shot her cord out of her right forefinger. It slithered across the scorched portico and snagged the door knob.

*"This door has a Keep-out spell."*

"Is the house not on fire, then? Are these flames a mirage?"

*"No, it burns. But the flames around this portal are magically enhanced."*

"Break that spell."

# Chapter Four

Abbie prepared to receive the after-effects of her cord breaking the spell and channeling the resultant magic into her. When it came, she recognized the distasteful stench of the Roman's ancient magic. It was the same as when Hafgufa dismantled his *Be-silent* spell over Figg.

Having the magic rush into her was always a horrid, invasive experience. This time was no different, but she was prepared for the influx and damped it down. Once home, the excess magical energy could be channeled into Klaus, her Grimm book, as a story.

Magic built up in her gut, flaming like an ulcer. Once Hafgufa broke the spell, Abbie had her unlock the door before retracting the cord.

The door led to a foyer. It was smoky inside the house, with flames climbing the walls, confirming this house was indeed on fire.

Her hand went to her back jeans pocket for her mobile to help her see through the smoking house. No back pocket. Or side pockets in her Regency gown. Abbie swallowed a curse.

A reticule hung off her left wrist. Could it be in there? She loosened the tie and snuck her hand inside. Her fingers encountered metallic edges and thrill shot up her spine. She flicked on the phone. No signal, but the battery worked. She touched the torch app.

There were several dead near the front door and windows, as if they'd been trying to escape and failed. A slender blade had stabbed many, while others had their throats mauled, likely by

Figg.

Swallowing her sorrow at their sad ends, she headed for the stairways. By the landing, she found a couple who lay dead. Sadness pressed down on her like a weighted blanket. These two were in formal dress, the man in a coat, breeches, and boots, and the woman in an expensive gown and slippers. They clung to each other, their throats torn and bloody.

Figg's work.

Could these two be the child's parents? If so, they were Abbie's relatives, too. That might explain why she was reacting strongly to them. Her Grimm instincts hummed at that assumption, suggesting she'd guessed accurately.

Throat clogged, she bid the couple a quiet rest in peace and sent up a prayer for all those littered around this home like discarded toys.

Time to find the girl. Clinging with desperation to her mother's words that the child was still alive inside this house, she raced down the stairs.

She stayed away from flaming rails and wallpaper and scaled over the burning steps. Her trip ended in a landing outside the kitchen. The smoke was less down here, and her flashlight outlined the view inside the hearth of this house.

People of all sizes and shapes–children, men, and women. All servants by their garb. All dead.

A timber crashed nearby, sparks and slivers flying by her. Despite Arthur's shield, Abbie recoiled.

The corridor outside the kitchen extended in two directions, leading to rooms. The child could be in any of them.

Swallowing her bile, she wiped her teary face and pulled out Levi. Callum had returned this to help her find her way back to him, but on this day, it might save a child.

She focused on the compass. "Levi, a girl's hiding somewhere nearby. She's related to me by blood. Can you locate her?"

The compass needles swung, calibrating between the North Pole and St. Michael's steeple, and then it added in the magical target - the missing child. Once the needles captured her location, Levi directed Abbie in succinct orders, spoken in a young boy's voice.

*"Go down the left corridor. Count four doors and open the one to your right."*

Following Levi's instructions, she found the room he indicated. A key hung from the lock, but the door was unlocked.

She entered and flashed her torchlight from one corner of the room to the other, slowly searching for a sign of the girl.

A gasp came from further in. The first sound of life she'd encountered, and the sweetest sound in the world.

"Hello? My name is Abigail–" she cut off before mentioning her last name. The less anyone from this time knew about who she was, the better. "I'm here to help."

Wherever the child hid, it had worked. The Roman had left empty-handed, because according to Levi and that involuntary gasp, the child was here. "You're safe."

This room looked to be a storage space, with shelves toppled and bottles broken. Red wine splashed across the floor like blood. After killing her parents upstairs, had the Roman followed the child down here?

No small footprints among the spilled wine carpeting the floor. No clue where she hid.

She had little time to spare and couldn't afford to have this terrified child scamper away in fear while she searched the room. Such a disaster would force Abbie to track her all around this burning house, wasting valuable time.

Abbie reached for the key on the outside. Pulling it out, she locked them both inside.

"I'm here to take you to safety." Abbie tucked the key into her reticule. "Who told you to come down here to hide?"

Silence. Then came a whisper. "Papa."

The child's parents must have stayed above to distract the monster from their girl. And paid a deadly price. The Roman had made it down here despite their valiant efforts.

*"Where is she, Levi?"*

*"To your left."*

"Who's with you?"

The child had heard Levi's response?

Of course. Unlike Levi, Hafgufa had no compunction about sharing Abbie's mental conversations with all nearby. She must have transmitted Levi's answer to the child.

This was one time, though, when she didn't mind the little girl hearing this conversation, because it might coax her out of hiding.

*"I didn't share."*

Hafgufa's response was a shock. She'd sort that out later. Her current focus was to get this girl out of hiding. "You heard Levi earlier. He is my compass. He helps me find people. What's your name?"

"Claire. Are you a fairy?"

Odd question. Ah, her roaming torchlight must have seemed like magic to a little girl who'd grown up in the 1800s.

Abbie had no inhibitions about lying to expedite a rescue. "Yes, I'm a fairy. Two more are waiting for us outside to take you someplace safe."

Silence greeted that explanation, and Abbie waited, holding her breath, fingers crossed.

"Mama and Papa said we're in danger." Claire's tone was sorrowful. "They said if they went to Heaven, not to worry because help would come, and I must hide until it did." Claire's next question came out tremulously. "Have they gone to live with God?"

Unable to lie to the child about this important fact, Abbie kept her tone gentle, but firm. "Yes, love. They are with God."

Claire whimpered; her cries soft inside her hidey-hole.

Abbie's chest tightened, and she wished she could give Claire time to grieve, but that could not be. It had grown warmer in the past few minutes. The fire could be catching up to them. Arthur would protect both her and this child from the fire, but dealing with a magical Roman or a giant Figg coming after them might be a harder feat. Time was not her friend. "Your parents would want you to come with me, Claire."

"Did God send you?" Claire hiccupped, her words slurring past her cries.

"Yes." Abbie was more certain of that now than ever. Why else would she and her family have landed here, in this time, in this place, right when Claire needed them most? "We're God's fairies." She stepped further into the room and held out her hand. "Will you come with me, Claire? We must hurry. We need to leave right now."

No response. Not even a question. Then a scraping came

from her left. She hurried in that direction and spotted a portion of the wall slide aside. A brown-haired girl poked her head out, like Alice in Wonderland coming out of a rabbit hole.

"Hello there." Abbie flashed her the most welcoming of smiles. Dropping Levi into her reticule, she helped Claire climb out. The girl was unusually heavy until Abbie spotted the leather valise she lugged. Claire was quite small, but that bag weighed her down.

Once Abbie set the child on her feet, she pointed to the bag. "What's all that?"

"It's mine. After giving it to me, Papa said I'm to never let go of it, ever."

"We'd better take that bag with us then, hadn't we?"

Claire nodded. "Yes, please."

"Well, we must hurry. That bag looks heavy, though. May I carry it for you?"

The girl shook her head vehemently and pulled the valise closer.

Abbie nodded. "Understood. How old are you, Claire?"

"Six."

A plus. She was likely to ask fewer questions at that age. At eight, Jimi questioned everything Abbie asked of him. "Do you trust me?"

The child nodded.

"Then close your eyes and allow me to carry you and your valise out of this house. It'll be smoky and loud outside this room. Ignore everything except what I say. All right?"

The child nodded and shut her eyes, hugging her valise.

*"Arthur, shields up around this girl, same as mine."*

Her ring flashed a light to the valise, using it as his

touchpoint, before the shield covered Claire. Once he buzzed to indicate he was done, Abbie picked up Claire.

Abbie hid her charge's face against her right shoulder and asked Hafgufa to help her with the weight of the child and her heavy bag. Unlocking the door, she ran out into a smoke-filled corridor. She raced toward the staircase, ducking around fallen timber and jumping over burning debris. Flames licked close. Arthur's shield kept them from getting burned.

She arrived at the staircase and discovered the fire had consumed most of the steps. No safe path to return the way she'd come. Through the kitchen, it would have to be.

There must be a door from there that led directly to the outside. A way for staff to enter here without going through the rest of the house.

She stepped over the fallen victims and hurried through the hollow shell of the kitchen. The kitchen's back door was also spelled. Working quickly, Abbie got through it. The door opened to stone stairs that led up to ground level. Carrying Claire, she raced up the stairs.

Once her feet touched the grassy lawn, Arthur shifted her shield back to normal and Abbie took her first full breath of clean, fresh air.

"You can open your eyes now." Abbie set the child down, heaving a relieved sigh. A quick check confirmed they had exited the back of the house. There was a vegetable garden on one side.

Abbie knelt beside the girl. Even with Hafgufa's help, it had been awkward carrying the girl and her valise. The case must be even harder for the child to lug about. "What's inside that, Claire?"

The child backed up, dragging her case, eyes wary. "It's a secret."

Considering that intriguing response, and that this child was likely Abbie's ancestor, she made an educated guess. She pulled Levi out of her reticule. "Do you have this in there?"

Claire's eyes widened. Then she flicked open the valise lid and searched inside. Abbie shone her mobile's light into the bag's dark interior.

"There it is!" She pulled out a compass that was a mirror of Abbie's artifact.

Family, indeed.

"Would you allow me to speak to the items inside?"

Claire frowned at her. "Like a Godfairy chat?"

Abbie's mood lightened at that odd phrase and her lips quivered, wanting to smile. Claire must have fused Abbie's earlier comments about her being a fairy and God sending her. Worked for her, so she nodded. "Yes, exactly. I want to have a Godfairy chat with your items."

"Very well." Claire pushed the bag toward Abbie, though she kept hold of the handle.

Abbie ran her hand over the opening. "Shhh. Now listen up. Claire needs to carry all of you, so I'd like each of you to be as light as you can, so she can do it with little effort. Can you do that?"

A hum of acknowledgment came from the items. Satisfied, she told Claire to shut the bag and bring it with her.

Claire nodded, lifting it. "Oh...it's easy to carry. Hardly anything at all."

"Good. Now let's go find my family."

The two of them raced to the front of the house.

On spotting them, Ruby and Margaret hurried over.

"You found her!" Abbie's mother embraced Claire and then Abbie.

"Claire, this is my mother, Margaret, and this is Ruby."

"Hello." Claire curtsied. "I'm pleased to meet two more godfairies."

"Two more what?" Though Ruby questioned Claire, her gaze scanned the horizon.

Searching for their enemy? Good reminder that they must get out of here fast. "I'll explain later. Time to bring out the carriage."

Ruby nodded and placed the pumpkin on the drive.

Claire *ooh'd* and *ah'd* when the carriage appeared, and then ran forward, hand extended to the foxes. Meanwhile, Margaret replaced Claire's and Abbie's burnt and soiled gowns with clean, less stinky ones.

"Oh, pretty." Claire twirled, admiring her new dress.

"Where are we going?" Margaret entered the carriage after Ruby. They sat side-by-side, leaving Claire and Abbie to sit facing them. Abbie glanced out the window. "The Roman might be waiting for us to come out the way we came in. We need another way out."

"There is only one lane leading in and out of here." Ruby sounded confident.

Nodding, Abbie knocked on the carriage wall. "Basil, can you make this carriage fly?"

Gigantic wings stretched out from either side of the carriage and the vehicle rose into the air.

"Ooh!" Kneeling on her seat, hands gripping the windowsill, Claire gazed out.

"Brilliant." Ruby breathed the word out, sounding as rapturous as Claire.

Abbie's mother merely gaped out her window.

"Basil, take us to the clearing where we first arrived. Fly high, in the clouds, so we're less likely to be seen." Abbie leaned forward and tapped her gran and mother's knees.

Margaret and Ruby aimed wide-eyed glances at her, and she tilted her head toward Claire. Her unspoken question: *What are we to do with this child?*

"We're not taking her with us to 1703." Margaret's tone was firm, but quiet, her rigid side glance aimed at her mother.

"I don't see why not." Ruby's eyes were lit up, as if her good mood at their flying hadn't dissipated. "She has three godfairies with her and a flying pumpkin carriage. She couldn't be safer."

Abbie tapped Claire's shoulder.

The child swung around from peering at the clouds passing by. "Yes, Godfairy Abbie?"

Abbie had to find someone to care for and protect the child she'd rescued. "Claire, what's your full name?"

"Claire Heidi Grimm."

Since Abbie's mother insisted this child was family, that last name wasn't a surprise. Of course, she was a Grimm. Dangerous to carry that name publicly, however. Abbie met and held her mother's and Ruby's gazes. "Her case contains magical artifacts. Before we leave, we must find someone trustworthy to take charge of her and give her a new identity."

Claire went back to staring out the window. Abbie lowered her voice. "Or the Roman will find her and that will be the end of our family line."

Abbie considered her options and then took out Levi.

"Where are Claire's closest relatives?"

The compass's levers spun and then stopped. *"France."*

Abbie sighed at that disappointing news. "It would take more time than we can spare to reach the continent, even in a flying carriage."

Margaret glanced outside. "Robert."

Abbie's pulse shot up. She leaned out to search below, half expecting to see him riding a horse. The landscape was bare. Nothing but greenery. Tense shoulders dropping, she slumped back and raised an eyebrow at her mother.

Margaret shrugged. "He's the only one we know around here whom we could trust with Claire's well-being."

"Mum." Abbie aimed for a reasonable tone. "Robert wouldn't recognize me. Also, he's due to be hanged in the next few weeks." Speaking those words was akin to having a rope slung around her neck. She raised a finger to her neck, half expecting to stroke a cord. Her throat was bare.

The carriage bounced once before rolling forward on the rough ground. They were back in the clearing where they'd first arrived.

The vehicle stopped, and the footman opened the door, unfolding the small wooden steps. Accepting his hand-assist, Abbie stepped outside.

Margaret followed her out, and then Claire.

Ruby exited last. "Peggy's idea has merit."

"You're just looking for a quick and easy way to get on with your journey." Abbie's snapped rejoinder spoke more of her darkening mood than genuine anger. Meeting Robert was a topic she wanted to avoid.

What would be the point of speaking to him? She wasn't

meant to save him, any more than all of her friends who had died in that London bombing. She shuddered as that realization sank in. Kali was right. Karma must work its will.

Ruby ended Basil's spell and collected her pumpkin as the animals and birds scattered. "Well, if Robert's out, how about we keep her? Once Claire comes into her talent, she'll have to learn about her life as a Grimm. Who better to teach her that than us, during a real-life mission?"

Abbie turned to Ruby, her back and shoulders rigid.

"What mission?" Margaret crossed her arms, her eyes narrowed, seeming as distrustful as Abbie.

"Since you're both against continuing to 1703, we could finish the villain off here. We know he's nearby and," Ruby pointed to Abbie, "you can track him using our compass."

Margaret's glance followed Claire, who was flitting around the clearing talking to bees and butterflies. "We can't take Claire into danger. And our enemy has Figg. We have no weapons."

"Whose fault is that?" Ruby stood, arms akimbo, narrowed gaze trained on Abbie.

"We will not finish the Roman off now or in 1703." Abbie flopped down onto the wild grass and gazed up at the blue sky. Robert was going to die soon and there wasn't a thing she could do to stop it. Mustn't do a thing. "We can't change history. Our every action might have a consequence that could be far-reaching. Our priority must be to safeguard Claire and then return home, so we disrupt nothing else. And we have less than a day to do so."

"I agree." Margaret sat beside her.

"Of course you would." Ruby set to pacing, swiping at tall

grass strands.

Claire ran and sprawled on her back, resting her head on Abbie's lap, her valise clutched between her arms.

Ruby strode closer to them, her gaze trained on Claire's bag. "There could be wish bombs in there."

"And if there are, they're going to stay in the bag." Abbie placed her arms protectively over the bag and Claire. Her gran was like a dog with a stick she refused to release.

# Chapter Five

"Now it's settled that we're not going after the Roman in this timeline," Margaret's smirk held not a hint of sympathy for Ruby, "let's discuss how Claire can join the Earl's household."

Abbie sighed deep and long at the return to this beleaguered topic.

"Mum, have you forgotten what happened to Pauline a year after Robert was hanged?" Abbie shook her head, hoping to end this talk once and for all. "Aside from this course of action only being a short-term solution, why would he or Pauline take Claire in? How could we convince them to be responsible for a child they've never met?"

"Think, Abbie." Her mother leaned her head on her fist to look at her. "If we persuade Robert's wife to become Claire's guardian, she might not succumb to heartbreak."

Abbie had hoped that at least she and her mother agreed they mustn't disrupt history. Was she alone in her views? "Where are you going with this?"

Ruby, who'd been wearing a morose expression, now tilted her head toward Margaret. "She means Pauline could have survived longer than newspaper accounts of the day show because she went into hiding with Claire."

Abbie's thoughts raced, playing out that possibility. "If Pauline has Claire to look after," Abbie stroked the child's hair, "she might find a reason to carry on."

"Godfairy Abbie, who is Pauline?" Claire had followed this adult conversation swirling around her.

"Pauline is Lady Ashford." She was so used to calling

Robert by his first name, she'd been doing it with his wife, too. That didn't suit Regency times. Would certainly not earn her any credits if she did so to the lady's face. "Lady Ashford is a talented sculptor, Claire. And, as you had to bid your parents goodbye today, she had to do the same to her daughter Lizzy."

If Lady Ashford and Claire could console each other, they wouldn't feel so lonely in the days and years to come. That's how the Standard Bearers had formed. To help each other through grief.

She stroked the child's hair. "As those who took care of us leave us, Claire, we must care for those who come into our lives next."

"Exactly!" Margaret nodded, as if the matter were settled. "That would be a much happier life for both of them. You must convince Robert to give you and Claire an introduction to his wife."

Now, this was a plan Abbie could get behind. Such a practical reason to speak to Robert when he was alive was irresistible. Heart pattering, Abbie sat up and took out Levi. "Locate Robert's position. Not his ghostly form, but the nobleman who is currently alive."

The compass needles twirled, and then they stilled. *"He's praying at St. Michael's church, Abbie."*

How appropriate.

"That's close." Margaret stood and dusted herself off. "Using the carriage, we could be there within minutes."

Claire jumped up, all smiles, valise in hand. "I love your flying carriage, Godfairy Abbie. And I want to meet Lady Ashford. Then she'll love me and take care of me like Mama."

Abbie's heart squeezed tight at her reasoning. In Claire's

heartfelt words, she sensed her grief inching closer.

"Let's walk to the lane and drive from there. The less flying we do in daylight, the better. Most people don't understand magic, Claire."

"Oh, poo!" The child slouched, but she followed Abbie toward the line of trees, beyond which was the nearest lane.

Abbie took her hand in sympathy. She, too, preferred to fly. It was faster and less bumpy than traveling on land, with the carriage having too little padding to accommodate for pitted roads.

Margaret and Ruby trudged after them through the bush. Once out of the brush, they waited for the lane to clear of traffic before Ruby transformed the pumpkin artifact.

They then drove to St. Michael's. They arrived to find the car park in front of the church was a dirt clearing where carriages could pull up. Another vehicle was already there. They lined up behind it.

The church was even more startling than for its lack of paving out front. All around the building, bushes were well-trimmed and cared for instead of growing wild. As for St. Michael's steeple, it stood ever so straight. Below that, three brilliant and colorful stained-glass windows depicted the story of Christ, from birth to death to resurrection.

Abbie hugged herself, taking in the building's majesty. Sunlight glinted off the depiction of an angel on the first panel. It was as if that angel were her guardian angel who'd visited Abbie several times now, signaling she was on the right track.

Claire made to get out, but Abbie held her back. "I want you to stay in the carriage with my mother, please." She didn't trust Ruby alone with Claire and that valise. "Ruby, you should come as my chaperone."

The child slouched back, eyes downcast, and her lips down-turned.

"She's a bossy boot." Ruby's muttered words stung Abbie, but made Claire giggle.

Ruby followed her out smiling, as if, despite her words of disparagement, she was glad to be chosen to attend to Abbie.

The two of them walked past the other carriage. It had an emblem on its door. Must be Robert's family crest. She trembled as it sank in that she was about to meet Robert. In the flesh!

She'd have to speak formally when they met. Do not repeat any of the curse words he taught you. Her lips spread wide as, one by one, she swatted back those naughty words.

She approached the church steps, her mind awhirl with what she would say and how it might feel to touch his hand.

Before she realized he had approached, a liveried man barred her way.

"Stand aside!" Ruby snapped the order, her tone regal.

Abbie started, as did the servant, his pupils widening.

The man blinked and then steeled himself. "His lordship, the Earl of Ashford, is inside." His tone grew more condescending with each word spoken. "By your leave, he requests a moment of privacy, ladies. You may enter after he leaves. He shan't be long."

"We are here to see his lordship." Ruby held her head high. "Kindly notify him he has visitors."

The man didn't budge. "You may approach his residence in Ashford and leave your card if you so wish."

They didn't have time for this. Abbie sent her cord

downward from her forefinger. A slender thread of gold, it was barely visible as it wrapped around his ankle.

The servant opened his mouth as if to speak and then he shut it, blinked a few times, and stood aside. "He will see you now." He bowed to Abbie.

She retracted her cord. "*Thank you, Hafgufa.*"

Ruby shot up an eyebrow in inquiry, but she followed Abbie without a spoken word. Her gran opened the door and only spoke after she'd shut it behind them. "You'll have to show me that trick sometime."

Never.

Hafgufa's ability to force a person to reveal secrets against their will could be deadly in Ruby's hand. This was the first time, however, when Abbie had used the cord to compel a physical action and imprint a mental suggestion *without* it making any conscious impression on the victim. The compulsion had worked remarkably well. She prayed she wouldn't have to use that trick on Robert. She desperately wanted his help, but she hoped he'd do it of his own volition, not because she forced him.

Yet, she knew little of *this* earl. The Earl of Ashford of 1816. How would he react to a stranger begging for help? He would be mourning his daughter. Also worried about what might happen to his wife once they arrested him. No wonder he was here praying for guidance. And she was about to pile on more trouble to his already full plate.

Abbie turned to Ruby. "I'd like to speak to him alone."

"Use the cord." Ruby must have sensed Abbie's unwillingness to do that.

Ignoring that advice, Abbie strode up the center aisle of

St. Michael's nave. On either side, benches and accompanying kneeling pads were in neat rows. The old earl from her time had removed those, as he had the stunning stained-glass panels before he sold the church to Abbie. Still, the familiarity of being inside St. Michael's settled the agitated butterflies in her tummy from a thunderous flutter to a quiet buzz.

Up ahead, below the rood, a man knelt, head bowed in prayer. Abbie would recognize Robert anywhere. He had an unmistakable aura of elegance and authority. As if he were born to lead. Before she'd reached halfway to his position, he raised his head and aimed a glare her way.

Not pleased to see me, Robert?

Abbie paused and waited for him to decide if he would come to her or if she must go to him.

In one swift move, he was on his feet, grabbing for his cane before he marched toward her with his distinctive limp. He was every inch the army major and nobleman, ready to lambast her for disturbing his peace.

Abbie bowed her head and curtsied. Her rehearsed words trembled on her lips and rang in her ears. *Good afternoon, my lord. I've come to speak to you about an urgent matter. I desperately need your wife to become the guardian of a child in dire straits.*

She rose and raised her head to meet his furious blue gaze. "Robert, I need your help."

Abbie gulped, a flush flaming her cheeks. She'd said the worst thing possible. She'd called him Robert.

He came to a startled halt, his gaze boring into hers.

She waited for him to order her to get out. Her cord twitched, but she clenched her right fist. *"No!"*

"We are unacquainted." He sounded uncertain, a frown line appearing between his brows. "Are we not?"

"We will be one day. You will become my staunchest defender. I wanted to be your forever friend, and instead, you became my champion."

A smile tilted his lips up, as if he were fighting the urge to laugh out loud. "So, you are the one I was asked to await."

"Asked by whom?" Abbie frowned. Who could have told him she was coming?

He pointed back to the altar. "I was up there praying. And had a vision of an angel who spoke one word. *WAIT.*" He chuckled. "I came to this church to beg for God's help. It seems, in His wisdom, he has sent me someone who needs my help instead." He bowed to her. "You now have my full attention, miss. What is this favor you wish me to grant?"

Joy bubbled inside her. He was still her Robert. He hadn't called his man to drag her out of here. At the least, she'd taken his mind off his dire worries for this moment. "My name is Abigail Grimshaw." The words tumbled out now. "I'm a Grimm who can see magic at work and interact with supernatural beings, like gods and demons."

"Demons?" Robert's voice spiked, as if that one word resonated.

"Yes, there may be an uprising in my time. But I'm here because a villain has been killing my family and other Grimms for centuries." She couldn't stop now she'd begun. "Today, he murdered the parents of a young girl whom we believe is part of our family line. We spirited her away, but we must return to our time, and we are afraid to leave her here unguarded."

"Your time?" He shook his head and glanced behind her at

Ruby. "How can I possibly help with such a dilemma?"

Abbie took a deep breath. "We were hoping Lady Ashford would take Claire into her home and heart as a ward. Our plan is for Claire to change her name and for Lady Ashford to go into hiding with her to keep them both safe, in case this villain comes after Claire again."

"You do not include me in your calculations." His tone dropped, his gaze sober, his focus now fully on her.

She shook her head, but couldn't bring herself to explain why. She didn't have to. He knew his fate. It showed on his face.

Finally, his adorable quirk of a smile returned. "I am to be your best ally?"

Abbie teared up. "Without exception."

"But not in my lifetime?"

Before she could respond, shouting came from outside.

"Wait here." Robert hurried to the entryway. He nodded to Ruby and then eased the front door open to glance out. Then he hurriedly shut and locked the door before limping back to Abbie. She hurried to meet him.

"Bow Street runners, accompanied by some locals. They are here to take me into custody. You know why?"

She nodded, a tear sliding down her cheek, leaving a hot, wet trail. "Yes."

"Good." He stepped closer, bringing his scent of rosemary, wax, and something else. Something real. Alive. A scent quintessentially Robert. "That will save a lot of explanations. Listen carefully." He instructed her on how she and her family could enter Ashford Castle without being seen.

*"Hafgufa, record these instructions, in case I forget a point or two."*

The cord buzzed her arm in acknowledgment.

Robert then told her how to convince his wife that he had sent Abbie.

Loud knocks pounded on the church door.

He held up his hand, ordering Ruby not to answer.

"There's one more thing I must convey." He gripped Abbie's upper arm, and in his rush, he likely did not realize the force he used. "You haven't inquired about this, but I have information that will come in useful in your time."

Abbie ignored the ache in her arm. "What is it?"

He indicated his lame leg. "This injury occurred during the Peninsula war."

"I know." She'd read about that, but had never probed Robert for more, waiting for him to tell her when he was ready. Seemed as if he was ready now.

"I can see I have neglected to share how the injury occurred. Else you would know what I'm about to say."

"He never... you've never talked about it. I've only read accounts of the war and those were skimpy."

More bangs sounded on the door.

Robert's gaze flicked to the church door before returning to her. "I made a pact with my comrades to never speak of this. But if you are likely to deal with a demon uprising, you must know what I know about the matter. A stray bullet or the strike of a rapier did not injure me. A demon clawed me in Spain."

Abbie raised her hand to her throat. Robert never spoke about his limp, but he had once mentioned fighting a demon uprising in Spain. When she probed, he wouldn't or couldn't elaborate.

"We fought them back and won." His words rushed out, as

if he sensed his time was almost up.

Abbie was shaking.

Keys jangled, and one sounded as if it had been inserted into the lock.

"You must hear this." Robert's tone was urgent, clipped. "Sending those demons packing involved a ritual. A priest conducted the ceremony. Every surviving soldier in my battalion donated a precious item to the cause of cleansing this world of that demonic infestation."

The door to the church banged open and men rushed in. They swarmed toward Robert.

Arms outstretched, Abbie barred them from him.

Robert gripped her hand, turned her around, and leaned in.

Men grabbed him, dragging him away.

Resisting their pull, Robert surged forward, his cheek scraping hers, and whispered a desperate message before he was drawn away.

The men jostled him out of St. Michael's church and Robert shouted over his shoulder. "Go to the Abbey of San Pedro de Siresa!"

Abbie ran after Robert, but Ruby caught up to her by the church landing before the steps, and held her back. "Abbie, we cannot change the course of this history."

"Let me go." Abbie struggled to free herself from Ruby's punishing grip. "I've already changed it by what I've told him. Besides, if both he and Pauline go into hiding together, it won't change anything."

"Yes, it will." Ruby's voice was hard and unrelenting. "If you save him now, he won't be the ghost you awaken."

That quieted her, and she stilled as Ruby's caution sank in. If the authorities didn't hang Robert for murder, his family would lay him properly beside his beloved wife and child. There would be no need to bury him in a forgotten portion of St. Michael's and she wouldn't have stumbled over his lost gravestone as a child of ten.

"You were right." Ruby's voice grew quiet and soothing. "I was mistaken."

Abbie shuddered. Ruby sounded so unlike her normally confident, assertive self.

"We mustn't change the past. Whatever happened, it happened out of that moment's need and necessity. We must allow history to progress as it did."

As she spoke, her gaze wasn't on Robert or Abbie, but on her daughter. Margaret peered out of their carriage window, looking pale.

"We all do the best we can." Ruby's contemplative voice lulled Abbie's agitation at Robert being bundled into his carriage. "We cannot now second-guess those decisions. All we can do is review past results to guide our future actions."

"Miss Grimshaw!" Robert's voice rang out, drawing Abbie's attention.

Catching his gaze, she mouthed her gut-wrenching apology for not saving him from his fate. *I'm sorry.*

He gave a brusque shake of his head, as if ordering her to *Buck up,* and not blame herself for his troubles. So like him.

Two runners held him in place inside the carriage, while another climbed up to sit beside the driver.

"When you return home, go to Spain." Robert's voice rang out as the carriage trundled away. "You might find what you need there."

She nodded to show she'd heard him.

He sat back, his head retreating inside the carriage, and waved a bound hand.

Abbie shuddered. "Ruby, if we send Lady Ashford into hiding with Claire, he'll be alone from now to the end."

"We don't know that for certain." Ruby's tone returned to its normal brisk manner, and her grip on Abbie loosened. "Not until we speak to his wife. Don't get ahead of yourself. Stay in this moment and reflect on the fact that you spoke to a man whom you admire and love. One who wasn't an ethereal shadow of who he used to be, but the real man. This was a rare opportunity, Abbie. Treasure it. Revel in it."

Abbie and Ruby stood on the church steps as Robert's carriage, with horses tied behind it, departed. Villagers followed on horseback, hooting victory calls.

Abbie was still trembling when Claire and Margaret climbed the steps to join her and Ruby on the church's landing.

"I'm sorry, love." Her mother's arms enveloped her and Abbie cried afresh. Claire joined her in sorrow, as if the child, too, was finally ready for that emotional release.

Abbie's group drove from the church and then trudged back on foot through the brush to reach their clearing, pumpkin artifact in hand.

Claire's face was still tear-streaked. This child had finally begun to grieve her parents' loss. A first step of many to come, before acceptance could truly sink in.

Abbie understood this process. It might take months or years to get over such a dear loss. She had gone through it when she lost her friends in London, and again today, when she let go of Robert's hand. Her throat closed in and she blinked rapidly to keep tears at bay.

Ruby stomped off into the woods. "I'm going hunting for our dinner."

Margaret took Claire by the hand. "There's farmland that way. Let's go scavenge vegetables for our evening meal."

Abbie appreciated the assist. She desperately needed alone time, and her mother could read her like a book.

Once on her own, she strolled around the patch of ground they'd chosen as their camp. Robert's eerie presence trailed her steps as she selected dry branches with which to build a fire or picked ripe red berries for their dessert.

# Chapter Six

Earlier, at the church, when Robert's cheek brushed Abbie's, his warmth had washed over her. His familiar scents poignantly paired with the unique aroma of a real Robert. If she scented his ghostly presence again at night, she'd remember him as he'd been today. His skin hadn't been half faded, but vibrant and glowing. His rich voice had resonated as he whispered his desperate plea. Now his words echoed, bringing a shiver to her heart, because it was as if their meeting today hadn't been their first true hello, but their final goodbye.

By the time her gran returned, Abbie had a fire burning, and had set aside a handful of washed strawberries snuggled on a bed of leaves for later consumption. Ruby dressed and cooked her kill on a makeshift spit. Without salt, the roasted rabbit turned out bland, but filling, alongside the carrots her mother and Claire had filched.

Despite it being summer, the night grew cool once their fire died out, making Abbie huddle into her many layers of clothing. Almost as warm as a blanket. The cloudy sky suggested that it might rain.

"Arthur, shield us while we sleep, including from the elements." That strengthened protection should keep them safe from predators, intruders, and bugs, as well as dry and warm despite any rainfall.

Arthur buzzed her in acknowledgment. *Tenting now.*

"We should head directly to Ashford Castle bright and early tomorrow morning." Ruby's tone was brisk and no-nonsense, as if she worried her family would delay her.

"It has to be earlier than that." Abbie lay back, gazing up at the night sky. No stars or moon visible tonight. The cloud cover was too thick. "We must be in Ashford before dawn."

"That's a long drive." Margaret came over to lie beside her. "Should we leave now?"

"No. It won't take us long if we fly. And we are less likely to be spotted in the dark."

"All right." Margaret lay on her side facing Abbie. "Then we can wash up and Marie-Jeanne can change us into clean clothes before we leave."

"Something in Claire's case could help us break into the castle." Ruby's gaze settled on the girl with a speculative narrowing. "The child needs to learn to use her artifacts. Best if she practices while we're here to guide her. It might even trigger her Grimm talents to manifest sooner."

Abbie glanced over at Claire. The child had been quiet all evening. Perhaps sensing Ruby's plans for her artifacts, she clutched the case to her chest.

"She's not ready yet." Abbie's Grimm instincts hummed in agreement with that assertion.

"That is a wise decision." Margaret tucked her head into Abbie's shoulder.

Claire came over and cuddled between them, the valise clutched in her arms. The bag poked into Abbie's side, but she was determined to live with that discomfort rather than give Ruby access to any wish bombs in there. Also, having Claire close by was like cuddling with Jimi and Nica. She shut her eyes, her lips tilting up in a bittersweet smile.

Ruby remained seated across the cold fire pit, morosely observing them. Finally, she lay where she'd sat.

Despite feeling content, sleep eluded Abbie. She adjusted to ease the pressure of the valise poking into her side, which became as much of an irritant as that figure of the older man inside the carriage with Figg. Who was he? So far, Kiros Hillier and Pyramus, two immortals, had been her prime suspects for being the Roman.

Lately, however, after meeting Pyramus, she'd tentatively crossed him off that short list. Kiros, his brother, was still there. His involvement was shaky because he was a black man, while the Roman Figg showed her and the fellow she'd seen in the carriage today were Caucasian.

Also, Ruby believed their enemy was human, not immortal. Abbie's glance flew to her gran. Ruby lay unmoving. Her even breaths suggested she'd fallen asleep. Abbie's instincts labeled that a ruse. Ruby was wide awake.

Abbie sighed at the conundrum that was her gran. Even after spending a full day in her company, she knew less about Ruby than before she landed in Abbie's kitchen, asking for help. Her gran had devoted her life to stopping their arch-enemy, so on some level, she had their best interests at heart. On that thought, her muscles relaxed and her eyelids grew heavy.

Today hadn't been a complete loss. Aside from sharing valuable information about how to reach his wife, Robert had also gifted her with a clue on how to defeat the Roman's plans for a demon uprising. She planned to follow up on the lead by traveling to Spain on her return home.

Would questioning her ghostly Robert about his injury unseal his vow to stay silent?

She clenched her fists as the day's events replayed of Robert being dragged away. Fresh sorrow crept closer, leaving her trembling in the cool night air. All thoughts of sleep fled, and she sat up, searching for a distraction. Her gaze fell on Ruby. Easing away from Claire, she tiptoed to where Ruby lay.

She sat cross-legged to face her gran. "You've met the Roman. What was he like?"

"He is a mage." Ruby's swift answer confirmed she was wide awake. "His specialty is disguises."

Ruby opened her eyes, but her gaze didn't meet Abbie's, as if she were deep in thought. "He's lengthened his life, and that of his killing tool, his dog, which is no simple spell. He has some extraordinary skills. Had. I'm certain he lost some ability after the wish bomb weakened his shield and that Grimm dagger pierced his flesh."

Abbie's admiration rose at Ruby's resolve and ingenuity in pursuing this powerful mage. "How did you find him?"

Ruby flashed a grin, her eyes sparkling with triumph as she finally met her gaze. "Instead of seeking him, I went back in time and checked old records about his Grimm kills. Ours is not the only Grimm family that kept an archive of their activities." She sat up, yawning and stretching her arms. "All Grimms are stellar record keepers."

"Show me?"

"Show you what?"

Abbie held out her right hand, and her cord slipped out of her forefinger. "What happened when you confronted him?"

Ruby stared at Abbie's invitation and then raised her left hand. Hafgufa slipped around her gran's wrist like a sparkling golden bracelet.

"I checked each place a Grimm had been killed, hoping to

find one where I could catch our enemy in the act."

As Ruby spoke, Hafgufa flashed Abbie a vision of Ruby coming across a dead, mangled body. She shuddered, baffled by the brutality of the killing. As if the Roman had held a personal grudge against his victim, except each Grimm he killed would have been a stranger to him.

"Each time, I was too late. Until 1703, when my timing was perfect. He was after a French Grimm. This time, I deliberately went early enough to befriend the Grimm. Then, together, we waited for the villain to present himself at the place and time when records showed this Grimm would die."

Abbie found herself at a shoreline with Ruby. A short, dark-haired man stood beside her gran. He held a glowing dagger while Ruby clutched a wish bomb. Confronting them was a young, tall, slender fellow with short, straight, black hair. He was in oriental garb. Was that a gold medallion on his chest?

"Hafgufa, I want a closer look at that pendant." Instantly, she was standing before the oriental gentleman, the amulet as clear as if she held it. A face was imprinted on it. Kiros? Why would this man be wearing an impression of the immortal Earth companion?

Abbie flew backward until she stood behind Ruby.

The East Asian bowed in greeting.

Ruby threw her wish bomb.

Her target deflected it with a magical shield that flared to meet the bomb. When the two collided, they both exploded. At that moment of contact, the French Grimm flung his dagger.

An agonizing cry rang out above the din of the explosion.

The blast threw Ruby and the French Grimm backward. He landed with a crunch and lay deathly still, his dagger back in his hand, but the weapon no longer glowed, and the blade was bloody. It must have struck its mark and maimed the Asian before returning to the Grimm's grip.

A storm erupted over the water, and the sky rumbled. A whirlwind swirled up from the sea.

"You started that cyclone!" Margaret's hard voice came from across the firepit.

Her mother had taken part in that vision. *"Hafgufa!"*

*"Not I."* Hafgufa's tone was rueful. *"I intended to share, but it was unnecessary."*

*"I don't understand."*

*"You are all Grimms. Each of you can all communicate with your artifacts, which includes me."* Hafgufa's tone then dropped to a whisper, as if she intentionally no longer broadcast her words. *"You have primacy, Abbie, as Grimm Guardian, but if the other Grimms wish to, they can see and hear your interaction with your artifacts. Unless you block that communication."*

"That cyclone was reputed to have killed thousands of innocents." Margaret still sounded gobsmacked, and rightfully so. Abbie, too, had been shocked when she first learned of Ruby's involvement.

"Collateral damage." Ruby gave a careless shrug, but her gaze was downcast.

Her mother gasped, sitting up, her gaze flinging daggers at Ruby. "How can you be so callous?"

Abbie held up her hand, and her mother clamped her mouth, swallowing further irate words.

Ruby's outstretched fingers were trembling. Abbie clasped

her gran's hand, retracting her cord. "This mage you attacked was East Asian."

"A disguise. After that dagger struck his chest, he transformed. Could have happened because he was badly injured. He may be a master of illusion, but in that moment, I saw his true self." Ruby snatched her hand back, clenching her fist. "I can identify him if I see him again without his disguise."

"I mainly noticed his amulet," Abbie mused.

"What amulet?" Margaret's question was filled with confusion. "All I noticed was that Ruby had bruised her head when she fell back."

"I didn't see the amulet or Godfairy Ruby fall." Claire's tone was steeped in sorrow. "Just all the fishies that died."

Margaret put an arm around the child.

Claire had shared in their vision. How curious.

"Are those fishies in heaven now, with Mama and Papa?" Claire's whisper came out in a teary voice.

"Yes, love, they are." Margaret held her close, rocking the child, before meeting Abbie's gaze above Claire's head.

Abbie nodded acknowledgment of her mother's unspoken message. Claire seeing what Abbie's cord had shown the rest of her family suggested something momentous.

The tragedy of Abbie's friends dying in that London bombing had triggered her Grimm senses to come to the fore. Claire's recent trauma must have done the same to her. Triggered her Grimm talent to manifest. That's why she'd heard Levi in her burning home. Why she could take part in this joint vision.

Most interesting was that Claire's focus had been on the creatures the wish bomb's explosion killed. The child's connection to animals, like her sympathy for the birds and animals who manned their carriage, were signs of how her Grimm talents were manifesting.

What a time in her life to be left alone with no Grimm to guide her. How could they abandon Claire to strangers, to norms? Who would teach her how to develop as a Grimm or, worse, what if, out of fear, her next guardian insisted she suppress her talent?

"We each saw what was important to us." Abbie's gaze roved to the child.

Claire wiped away her tears, her gaze flitting from Ruby to Abbie. She was following this conversation closely.

"Why?" Ruby wrapped her arms around her knees. "What was the purpose of showing you three different parts of what I went through?"

"We focused on what our Grimm senses are attuned to. Claire noticed the aquatic animals that were affected. Mum's focus was on family matters. Your head injury. Since your talent is foresight, Ruby, your Grimm senses showed you that the Roman had been injured enough to affect his future."

Her cord buzzed her arm in agreement with her assessment. "I learned what I needed to complete my mission as Grimm Guardian. The amulet with Kiros's image on it. Though I'm uncertain about the significance of that information."

Still rocking Claire, Margaret caught Abbie's gaze. "I've read about such amulets. Covered in gold leaf, they often depict a parent and act as birthing gifts among Romans."

"That means that the enemy we seek might be Kiros's child." Abbie's pulse sped up at that possibility. One more item to add to her to-do list after she returned home. Speak to Kiros.

"If the Roman is his son, then Ruby is correct. The Roman is not immortal. According to Kiros, their children do not inherit their immortality."

"*If* he was telling the truth." Her mother cautioned, releasing a squirming Claire. The child's eyes looked sunken, and her tear-stained face was strained. It had been a long and stressful day for all of them, but especially for this little one. Time they all rested before they set off for Ashford.

Abbie faced Ruby. "Thank you for sharing that story about your confrontation with the Roman."

Ruby stretched her fingers and rolled her wrist. "That's quite the cord."

Abbie couldn't agree more. "Goodnight." She returned to lie beside Claire and her mother. Claire's slender arm wrapped around Abbie's waist.

Before long, Ruby joined them on Abbie's free side. At that positive sign they were on this adventure together, Abbie took Ruby's icy hand.

Her gran gave her fingers a gentle squeeze before releasing it and turning over.

Soon, everyone's breathing grew heavy and regular, suggesting Abbie's family had fallen asleep. Not so her. She lay awake, her thoughts racing.

She had learned a vital piece of information about Kiros's relationship to the Roman. They might be father and son. Would explain why he'd lied to protect the villain. He'd even thrown his brother under the proverbial bus to do so, implying Pyramus was responsible for the London bombing.

The Roman had magically enhanced the length of his life and Figg's. Which led to an uncomfortable question. If Figg had been so useful for centuries, why had he abandoned the dog two years ago?

After Abbie had a chat with Figg using her cord, could the dog have done as she'd requested and refused to kill on command? The only ones he'd killed since then were demons, and that had been to protect Callum. If Figg refused to kill for the Roman, the pup would be useless to him. Could that be why he'd abandoned the dog?

What hadn't he killed Figg? He'd had no compunction about hurting the dog. He'd blinded Figg in one eye out of petty revenge for the dog failing to kill Abbie.

Unless, as her gran asserted, the Roman was no longer as strong a mage. Figg was not only spelled to live a long life, but he had the power to transform into a giant, murderous creature. Could the dog now be too powerful for the Roman to kill? Had it been easier to let Figg loose into an unsuspecting populace? He wanted to release demons into Earth's human population. So, why not a killer dog?

Had he ever wondered why there were no viral reports of a killing dog on the loose in Kent? Or had he given Figg little thought after the dog was no longer of use? If so, advantage Callum and Figg.

On that happier note, murmuring a silent, *Wake me an hour before sunrise,* Abbie fell asleep.

It was still dark when Abbie opened her crusty eyelids. Waves of warmth flowed from a fire. Ruby sat on the other side of the flames, but her mother and Claire were absent. Abbie rubbed her eyes, cleaning them and blinking away the remnants of her sleep. She might as well have just fallen asleep. If she was awake, though, it must be close to sunrise.

*"An hour from sunrise, as requested."*

Hafgufa's response had Abbie sitting up, wide awake. Had she used the goddess as her alarm clock? She barely remembered making the request. Heat crept up her cheeks at her impertinence. *"Sorry."*

*"You are never alone."* Hafgufa's familiar refrain was welcome, but, this time, the cord's tone had been affectionate. So unlike the usually gruff water goddess.

"The child's gone with Peggy to wash up at the stream." Ruby's smirk drew Abbie's attention. "Claire took along her valise. If I wanted to get my hands on what's inside that bag, I could have last night. All three of you slept so soundly, nothing would have woken you bar a wish bomb going off."

That reminded Abbie that Arthur's powers weren't endless. He'd been active all day yesterday and all night, keeping them safe. Best to save him for an emergency.

*"Arthur, you'd better power down and rest."*

Her ring acknowledged the suggestion and the link between the ring on her finger and her family cut off.

Abbie stood and brushed dirt and leaves off her gown before walking over to where Ruby cooked quail eggs. She had cracked them over hot flat rocks beside the fire.

Abbie had a question she'd been meaning to ask her. "When we were by the church, you said you had realized we should not alter history. Explain." That was completely counter to what Ruby had been doing since she stole that hourglass from Abbie.

Ruby flicked her an assessing glance and then her gaze swerved to study the bush. Was she looking for Margaret?

"I've made decisions I regret. Most prominent among them

was leaving Peggy."

A smile teased Abbie's lips at the heartfelt admission. "You should tell her."

"Would she believe me?"

"She knows you better now."

"I doubt that helped." Ruby's mouth turned down.

"She might surprise you. You're growing on me, and I'm my mother's daughter, through and through."

A harsh laugh slipped out of her gran. "You're nothing like Peggy."

At Abbie's raised eyebrow, Ruby shrugged. "She's fierce, while you're a willow that bends at the slightest breeze. Peggy's determined. You allow every Tom, Dick, and Harry to influence your every decision. While she's passionate, giving her complete love to those she cares for, you guard your heart as if it were the crown jewels."

"I do not!" Abbie sat back, arms crossed, chin raised. If by Tom, Dick, and Harry, she meant her Standard Bearers, that was valid enough, but not the rest.

"Then, why haven't you tried to bed the good ghostly earl?" Ruby flashed her a wicked grin. "Don't tell me you've never fantasized about him? I wouldn't believe you."

"Robert is married!"

"Technically, he hasn't been married for over two hundred years. Till death do us part? As for the copper, you've found every excuse to keep DCI Callum Radford at arm's length."

"Figg–"

Her gran cut her off with a swipe of her hand. "Figg is a dog. One you could have disposed of whenever you wished with your god-killing cord. So, not a genuine threat. Keeping the dog alive is an excuse to hold Radford off at arm's length."

Ruby was on a roll, either missing or ignoring all warning signs that her words were not well received. "If you can't be honest with me, Abbie, at least show yourself that courtesy."

Abbie took a deep, calming breath. She didn't need to justify her actions. All this vitriol was Ruby's way of changing the subject. They'd been discussing her shortcomings, not Abbie's.

# Chapter Seven

Abbie faced Ruby, her chin lifting with determination. "Do me the courtesy of getting back to my original question. Why do you now value preserving history?"

"I might have been a little obsessed with killing our enemy," she met Abbie's glance, "because I blamed him for ruining my life. Yesterday, when I insisted you allow the earl to face his fate, I realized I hadn't done the same."

"Go on."

"I've been blaming our enemy for keeping me from Peggy. But I chose to go after him. Just as you choose to keep your DCI at arm's length. In both cases, our fault lies with us for not prioritizing the ones we love. I allowed my fury at losing my husband to blind me to my responsibility to my girl. The experience taught me a harsh lesson. For those without power, it's too dangerous to be around a Grimm. I'll never fall in love with a human again. It's too easy to lose them."

"Gramps was a norm?" Like Callum. Like Abbie's dad.

"Yes." Ruby's face grew somber. "To be fair, I would never trust a supernatural enough to give him my hand, either. So, I devoted my life to hunting our enemy."

Sounded like a life sentence for a lonely existence. Unable to find the words to convince Ruby to consider a different path, Abbie stood to wash up. If they didn't leave soon, they'd be too late to catch Pauline where Robert said they'd find her at dawn.

She turned back with a last question. "Why do you keep calling Mum, Peggy?"

Her gran released a deep sigh and stayed silent.

Abbie took a defeated step away.

"The night I conceived my daughter," Ruby's voice was melancholic, "Peggy Lee's *Fever* was playing on the radio. It was the last time I was with my husband before the Grimm killer murdered him while trying to kill me. I fled and hid, leaving behind all but our artifacts. Once I learned I was with child, in my heart, she became Peggy. That was all I had left of my love. That name reminds me she's a part of both of us."

"Hoy!" The shout came from the bushes before Claire rushed out, followed by Margaret.

"Time to wash." Abbie offered Ruby a hand. "Coming?"

"Already done. I'm an early riser."

Abbie left her, looking forward to a bit of privacy to think over Ruby's words. Her gran was mistaken about most of what she said, but she had made one valid point. Abbie had kept Callum at arm's length, even after they started dating. Thinking of him brought a hot flush to her cheeks, and other than a quick wave to her mother and Claire, she hurried past, head bowed.

"All okay?" Margaret turned to watch her.

Abbie nodded. "Mum, ask Ruby why she keeps calling you Peggy." She hurried away before her mother could probe about her troubled state.

Thoughts about Callum dogged her steps. However, once she reached the softly flowing stream, it was Robert who stared back at her from her reflection in the water.

The day she ran through the woods when she was ten and stumbled over his gravestone, she had concluded one thing. That he must be terribly lonely. It could have been her latent Grimm instincts that had given her that insight.

As a grown woman of twenty-four, Abbie had moved Robert's grave to rest beside the bones of his daughter and wife. His sincere gratitude had cemented that earlier impression. Robert was profoundly lonely without his family.

Yesterday, he had whispered a desperate plea. He'd begged Abbie to impress upon his wife that she should live a full life after he was gone. That wish must have been born out of his need that Pauline be gifted a less lonely existence than the one he now envisioned for himself. Especially after Abbie spilled about how he wouldn't survive his current dilemma to be available to protect Claire.

A quote from Jane Austen rang in her mind, changed to fit Robert's situation. It was her answer to Ruby's question about why she'd never made a play for him.

*His heart is, and always will be, Pauline's.*

She cupped the cold river water and splashed her fiery face. Flicking away water droplets, her fingers cold and trembling, she returned to her family.

They had a quick breakfast of fried eggs. Like their dinner, the meal was bland, but filling. Her mother and Ruby stayed silent, sitting far apart. Ruby must have rebuffed Margaret's question about why she called her Peggy.

Ruby set the pumpkin on the ground and activated it, while Abbie and her mother stomped out the fire. Claire ran to pet the returning foxes and birds.

Ruby knew more about Grimms, and how their talents might manifest. After all, unlike Abbie and her mother, a Grimm parent had raised Ruby. She'd also researched their kind from around the world while tracking down their enemy. "What can we do about Claire coming into her Grimm heritage?"

Ruby glanced over at the child with a narrowed gaze. "She'll need guidance as she takes up her legacy."

"Good thing she won't have to rely on you for that, then, isn't it?" Margaret's bitterness layered her words as she accepted the footman's help to enter the carriage. Claire followed her in.

A flush colored Ruby's cheeks, but she didn't say another word.

Abbie climbed in next, suppressing a sigh. This was going to be a tense trip. Ruby entered last.

Margaret had sat Claire beside her, facing forward. That forced Ruby to sit beside Abbie, facing her daughter. Unsatisfied with the arrangement, Ruby gestured imperatively for Abbie to climb over her. Once they switched places, Ruby observed the child and her valise with a brooding gaze, earning a thunderous frown from Abbie's mother.

Swinging her legs, Claire smiled at Ruby sweetly.

Abbie tapped the carriage. "Basil, fly us to Ashford castle."

As the carriage rose into the air, Claire knelt in her seat to look out. Giant, dark wings flapped in the cool night air.

Her mother adjusted a shawl Marie-Jeanne had added to her outfit. "What if we're seen?"

Abbie glanced out the window. "It's dark enough, and we have no lights to show our passage. Only a few folks are about and too focused on their tasks to notice us. Everyone else is likely still abed."

The view below, of dark gray fields, rooftops clustered together like chickens roosting, and the occasional church steeple left her breathless. This was her country, her small place in this world. Her land to guard.

Heart thumping quicker and her fingers gripping the rough window ledge, Abbie searched the lanes below for a dark carriage, picturing their enemy out hunting for Claire. Wherever he was, he remained well hidden. She sat back, lips pursed. Just as well. Best if they met Lady Ashford without a crisis dogging their heels. Especially with Claire along.

"What did Robert tell you about his wife?" Her mother's question took Abbie to the meeting in St. Michael's church. "Anything that can help us?"

"Her studio is in the northeast tower."

Claire abandoned her sky-watching to turn and follow Abbie's storyteller voice. A smile teased Abbie's insides at that abrupt change in interest. She was a Grimm child. None of them could resist storytelling.

"Lady Ashford's sculpting studio is her sanctuary. No one disturbs her while she works there in the early mornings. He said that will give us a private place to meet and talk."

"Could I be a sculptor when I grow up?" Claire's tone was wistful, her hand running down the valise's handle.

"You can be anything you want." Ruby's tone was brisk. "As long as it doesn't take time from your calling."

"What's a calling?" Claire frowned, her head tilted.

"You're a Grimm. That's your calling."

Margaret took Claire's hand. "Unless you decide you want to be something else."

"You can't ever choose to be something else." Ruby now caught Margaret's gaze and held it. "If you do, you'd be lying to yourself."

The tension inside the carriage flared. Her mother looked away first.

Time to change the subject. "What should I say to Lady Ashford?"

"You'll know exactly the right thing to say." Margaret's shoulders relaxed. "You always do."

"Thanks, Mum. This time, I'm unsure about that."

"Maybe the shell can help." Claire opened up her valise to look inside.

Abbie wanted to hug this little girl who had lost so much, but still wanted to help her. "What shell?"

"Papa always listened to it when he didn't know what to do." She pulled out a large seashell and extended it toward Abbie. "Here. You try."

Abbie took the seashell, but her thoughts were on Claire's words about her father. This was the second time the child had connected her father to the artifacts. First, he'd asked her to guard the family artifacts. Now it sounded as if he had been the Grimm who could hear this seashell speak.

If Claire was related to their family, could this mean that she was the first female Grimm in their line? Or were both parents Grimms?

"Did your mama ever use this seashell, Claire, or any of the other artifacts in your valise?"

The girl shook her head, eyes lowering, her fingers twisting around each other. "Only Papa used them."

Abbie met Ruby's and then her mother's gaze, and both ladies nodded their heads to show they followed her thinking on this matter. A theory to test later, for Claire appeared downcast at this reminder of her parents. So, Abbie focused on the seashell instead.

The size of her hand, the shell was smooth and cool to

the touch. She recalled seeing this in her rucksack, but had never called on it. Klaus's records noted this artifact as a fortunetelling tool. Since Abbie relied on her Grimm instincts to guide her, she'd never felt the need to call on this item. "Have you ever listened to it, Claire?"

The girl nodded. "When I hid inside the wall, there was a lot of banging in the room and then a man shouted at me to come out. I put the shell to my ear and asked what I should do. It said, *Stay.* Then, when you came, it said, *Go.*"

Smart shell. Abbie held the artifact up to her ear. "What should I say to Lady Ashford?"

A hollow sound came from inside the shell, as if a wave flowed toward her. *"Tell her to seek out her love."*

Abbie shuddered at what that answer implied.

"What did it say?" Her mother raised an eyebrow.

Hadn't she heard the answer? She'd been able to hear Hafgufa last night.

*"Answer only to Grimm speaker."* The shell's tone was unyielding.

Ah! Her cord could learn a thing or two from this shell about privacy.

Hafgufa gave her forearm a twinge for that rebuke.

Abbie suppressed a mischievous chuckle and handed the shell back to Claire.

Ruby intercepted the transfer. "Would you mind if I ask it a question, Claire?"

The child frowned, and then nodded. "All right."

Ruby put the shell to her ear and shut her eyes. She didn't say her question aloud. When Ruby snapped open her eyes, she trained her gaze on Claire before she swerved to observe

Margaret. Then, slowly, she returned her gaze to Claire and handed the shell back.

"Do you want to try, Godfairy Margaret?" Claire offered the shell to Abbie's mother.

Margaret hesitated and then shook her head. "I don't have a question I need answering."

The child shrugged and tucked the shell back into her valise and snapped the case shut.

"What did the shell advise you?" Ruby turned to Abbie, a frown between her brows.

"I want to think about it before sharing. You?"

"Same." Ruby gazed out the window, hands clasped so tight that her knuckles were white.

Abbie and her family arrived in Ashford while the sky was still dark. Below, Ashford Castle's four majestic towers and its surrounding moat presented a spectacular view.

"According to Robert, on awakening, Pauline strolls in the rose garden before heading to her studio to sculpt."

Margaret glanced out the window. "I don't see her."

"It's not quite sunrise yet." Abbie, like the rest of her family members, could barely stay seated as they gazed down at the castle. Along the south wall, a long, narrow garden was used to grow herbs and other produce. The flower gardens seemed to be all along the south and east sides. The bailey had formal garden hedges. Gatehouse doors, barred for the night, were housed in that north wall, with the drawbridge drawn up.

She tapped the side of the carriage to catch Basil's attention. "Take us down to the wooded area on the east of this castle, please." She turned to her family. "That's how Robert said we should approach his home. It's how we can speak to his wife in private, with no one knowing we're here."

The carriage landed and trundled to a halt. They'd agreed that taking the pumpkin with them would give them the flexibility to leave from wherever they ended up, instead of returning here. So, once they disembarked, Ruby changed the carriage back to its tiny pumpkin size and released the animals and birds.

"We should keep an eye on the time." Margaret's gaze was on the path that led into the woods. "The travel spell only lasts twenty-four hours, right?"

Ruby pulled out the hourglass. "There's less than a quarter of the white grains still to fall."

"I'd say we only have a handful of hours left." Abbie frowned as Ruby tucked the hourglass back into her bosom. "We still have so much to accomplish."

"Let's be quick then." Ruby set off down the path at a brisk pace.

"Where are we going after here?" Claire skipped along beside Ruby.

Abbie was right behind Claire and answered. "We're hoping you can stay with Lady Ashford."

"No!" Claire came to a crashing halt and swung around to glare at Abbie. "I want to go with all of you."

Before Abbie could console her, Ruby took her hand. "I won't leave you. Come along."

Abbie frowned at Ruby's rash words. She didn't condone lying to Claire about her future.

Her mother shook her head, took Abbie's elbow, and held her in place, allowing Claire and Ruby to walk on ahead. "Leave it be."

"Lying to Claire in this instance doesn't help. It only delays the inevitable."

"Ruby isn't planning to say goodbye to Claire."

Was this her mother's Grimm instinct about family matters coming into play? If so, she disagreed with Ruby's decision. "Claire can't come with us, and if Ruby thinks I'm leaving her behind in this time, she can think again."

"Claire needs taking care of." Her mother walked on.

"That's why we're going to enlist Pauline's help." Abbie lifted her skirts and hurried after her mother.

"She needs a Grimm." Her mother's tone was firm, and her steps steady. "I wish I'd had my mother's help in understanding my role. I should have done that for you, instead of keeping you in the dark so long about your heritage."

This was the first time her mother had even hinted that she regretted not telling Abbie the truth about her Grimm legacy. "You did what you thought was the best for me."

Was this what worried her mother? Abbie slung her arm around Margaret's waist. "You won't lose Ruby again."

Margaret shook her head, but looked teary. "She was never meant to be mine."

Abbie paced her mother's faster steps as they attempted to catch up with the two up ahead. "You gave up your role as a Grimm to care for me, and you had Dad to help you raise all of us. I can't see Ruby giving up being a Grimm, even if she has a child to look after. I strenuously oppose her staying here."

Up ahead, a building came into view behind the cover of trees.

"Stop!" her mother spoke in a dead whisper.

Abbie wasn't sure how, but both Ruby and Claire turned

and raced back to them.

"What's wrong?" Abbie swung around, half expecting to see the Roman behind them.

"There's danger ahead." Margaret's voice filled with dread.

"I agree." Ruby pointed toward the castle, whose towers were visible above the treetops. "Our enemy is headed there. I sense his approach."

"Arthur, shields up over all four of us." The ring's energy vibrated around her and Abbie sighed in relief.

Her mother turned to Claire. "Might also be worth getting out one of those wish bombs from that valise."

"Seriously?" Abbie couldn't believe those words had come from her mother instead of Ruby.

Ruby swung to Claire. "Will you give us one of the wish bombs? The man who killed your parents needs to be stopped."

"No!" Abbie placed her hand over Claire's shoulder. "Leave it in there."

"Abbie!" Her mother snapped her name out like a whip. "This is no time to quibble about the bomb. If ever we need to use it, it's now."

"We are not taking him out in this timeline." Abbie swiped a hand. "According to history, Lady Ashford will be fine, at least for another year. Our best course is to reach her before the Roman, and extend her Arthur's protection."

She prayed she wasn't about to get Robert's wife killed by her decision not to harm their enemy in this timeline. Yet, the thought of losing either Figg or Callum or her children because of the changes to history she made now was unthinkable.

She held up her hand when both Ruby and Margaret opened their mouths as if ready to argue. "All we need to do in this timeline is to identify him, so we can take him out in my time. Our priority is to keep Claire safe, nothing more."

"Ahrrr!" Ruby growled, before taking Claire's hand and hurrying toward the shed. She flung open the door, banging it against the wall. "You are such a pacifist." Ruby sneered and waved Abbie ahead. "I don't see how you have any Grimm blood in you."

Abbie entered the shed, sliding a finger down the rickety door. How had that wood withstood Ruby's violent treatment without falling apart? The shed's inside was quite large, longer than wide. About the size of a small house. She headed to the far end.

She called over her mother and Claire. Together, they shifted aside several empty crates until they uncovered a faded carpet. Pulling that aside, revealed a floor that was worn. If she hadn't known where to look, she'd never have spotted the slight indentation on a board.

She pressed that depression, and a lock clicked. She lifted the trapdoor to reveal an opening.

Abbie asked Arthur to brighten all their shields before they descended into that dark hole. Once a gentle glow appeared surrounding each of them, in a trice they were down the ladder. They landed in a tunnel that stretched out to one side. As her eyes adjusted to the darkness, shadows within shadows became clearer.

# Chapter Eight

Ruby took the lead inside the tunnel. The passageway sloped downward and then leveled out. Shivering in the muggy air, Abbie suspected they now traversed beneath the moat. Her heart pounded the whole while.

This tunnel was wet and moss-covered to the touch, but solid enough to not collapse in on them. No one spoke until the floor sloped upward.

"We approach the castle." Ruby's voice was pitched higher than normal. Abbie wasn't certain if she spoke from an educated guess or from tapping into her Grimm instincts.

By the time they reached a dead end, they were panting, as if they'd all jogged here without conscious thought.

The glow of Arthur's shield highlighted a ladder rung. It was at least ten feet above her head. She shot her cord upward to snag the lowest rung and tugged. The ladder slid toward her in a clatter.

"I'll go first." Abbie stood before the ladder. "Claire, you come after me. Mum and Ruby, you two come up last to ensure no one ambushes us from below."

At their nods of agreement, she hiked up her skirts to ease her climb. The edges of her skirts felt damp as she tied them. The rungs of the wooden ladder were cold to the touch and slippery, but solid enough to hold her weight. She headed up and up. Just when Abbie thought she couldn't climb one more rung, the edges of a doorway appeared straight ahead.

"Arthur, reduce our shield glows." She then knocked on the door. Three rapid taps, followed by a pause, and then one tap, another pause, and two more taps. It was Robert's signal to his wife that he was on the other side of a door. He'd assured her that Pauline would recognize that combination.

Footsteps hurried toward her on the other side of the door, and then it sounded as if items were being dragged across the floor. A lock clicked, but the door didn't open.

"Who is there?" That woman's voice was pitched high, quick, and layered with hope.

"Hello. Robert sent us."

Silence greeted her response.

"Who are you?"

It had to be Robert's wife on the other side. Who else would have recognized the knock enough to unlock the door?

"I'm Abigail Grimshaw. I'm here because I need your help, Lady Ashford. Robert told me how to get here. About your secret signal. He sends his love. Will you let me in?"

There was a scuffle of footsteps as if the lady retreated. "You may enter."

Abbie tentatively pushed the door open. Creaking a little, it swung inward.

"Where is my Robert?"

Abbie had opened a door positioned on a wall. Hard to see who spoke to her past the blinding light that flooded the room. "He's not with us." Abbie blinked to clear her sight.

The lady finally came into focus—a pretty brunette in a blue empire-waisted gown covered in a full-length brown dusty apron. She held a hammer in one hand, a chisel in the other, and a white cap protected her hair. The sculptor, the artist, and the love of Robert's life confronted Abbie with a mixture of fear and hope.

"I bring news." Abbie offered her hostess a tentative smile.

The lady lowered her hand that held the chisel, but not the one gripping the hammer. "Where is my husband?"

"On orders of a magistrate," Abbie gentled her tone, if not her words, "Bow Street runners came to fetch your husband at St. Michael's yesterday. I came as soon as I could."

Pauline gasped, and then she teared up.

"I'm sorry to come with such bad news." Abbie stayed put inside the tunnel and counted down ten seconds. Her mother believed that's how long it took to gain control of rampant emotions, and Pauline was in the throes of the shocking news Abbie had delivered.

Inside the room, morning light bathed the space. Dawn had arrived while they'd been in the tunnel. In the center of the room, Pauline stood behind a work table. Chairs were stacked against the far wall, while several blocks of stone and a couple of statues, appearing as still as their sculptor, were stationed before a row of tall sash windows.

The sheer brightness haloed a frozen Pauline, gripping the chisel and hammer as if they were weapons instead of working tools. Despite their using Robert's secret knock, this lady stood on guard. *Good on her.* She'd need that fighting spirit to face what was to come.

"That he will not be returning to me is hard to accept." Pauline's shaky voice broke the silence. "Who are you? How are you acquainted with my husband?"

Lifting her skirts, Abbie took her first tentative step into the room from the wall opening. "Robert sent us to gain your assistance. He gave us this secret way to enter your studio and shared your private knock sequence to convince you we mean you no harm."

"We?" Pauline frowned at her.

"I'm here with two women and a child."

"They're my godfairies." Claire's voice came from the opening behind Abbie. Then the child's face came into view through the wall opening. Abbie moved aside and Claire, still hugging her valise, jumped down to the floor of the studio. "They can do magic!"

"This is Claire." Abbie placed a restraining hand on the girl's shoulder before she blurted out their secrets too soon.

Her gaze fixed on Claire, Pauline set her hammer and chisel on her work table. Her wide-eyed gaze stayed on the little girl and softened. "How old is she?"

Rather than sharing her guess, Abbie tapped the girl's shoulder. "Claire, tell Lady Ashford your age."

"Six summers, my lady." Claire curtsied.

"Hello, Claire." Pauline came around the table. "I am pleased to make your acquaintance."

Ruby and then Margaret stepped into the studio, shutting that door, which now looked to be an uninterrupted wallpapered wall.

"My godfairies say you're to be my guardian." Claire moved closer to Pauline, studying the dusty marks on the lady's apron with interest. "Is that true?"

Pauline turned a stunned gaze to Abbie and the two other women in her studio.

Abbie shrugged. "We hope so."

"That you are her godfairies?" Pauline's lips quirked in the first hint of a smile.

"That you'll take guardianship of Claire." Abbie warmed

to this woman. Even in this dire situation, her sense of humor shone through.

"It is too early for this conversation." Pauline's smile vanished. "I've not breakfasted yet. Have you?"

"No, we're starved." Ruby brushed the dirt off her skirt. "All we've consumed since last night are quail eggs."

"We had some delicious stolen carrots for supper." Claire moved to the sculptures, fingering a roughly hewn statue of what might be a milkmaid, carrying a bucket.

"Along with a roasted rabbit that Ruby caught and dressed for us." Abbie pointed a thumb at her gran.

"With sweet strawberries." Margaret offered. "My daughter scrounged those in the woods."

Pauline pointed Claire to a bowl of water on a sideboard. "You may wash up over there."

"I washed this morning." Claire showed Pauline her hands, and then she frowned. "They were clean when we left."

"I'm sure they were." Pauline stroked Claire's hair before making her way across the room to pull a cord by the mantlepiece. "You'd best wash up again before you eat. Sounds as if you four have been on an adventure."

Abbie took her turn at the washbasin after Claire. Her mother and Ruby followed suit. Pauline offered them towels.

Abbie discreetly shut the large double doors that led out into a corridor. They appeared tall enough to allow easy passage of large blocks of stone in and out, as Pauline completed her sculptures.

Robert's love for his wife was in every facet of this studio. Abbie bet he had arranged for the extra-large door installation, as well as for all those east-facing windows in his wife's studio.

She turned to Pauline. "We have much to talk about. In private."

The lady shuddered, holding onto herself as if afraid she'd fall apart otherwise. "Robert did not want me to see him taken into custody. I suspect that's why he went to St. Michael's. He must have known they would come for him soon." Pauline's last words hitched.

Abbie's mother hurried over and took her hand. "You will need to be strong for him, my lady."

"And for Claire." Ruby's tone was firm as she walked over and draped her arm around the young girl.

Pauline's gaze swerved to Claire, and her lips trembled. She pulled out a tall stool beside the work table and sat. "Tell me your story."

"I warn you, it will sound outlandish." Abbie stared at the lady, assessing her. If they told her the truth, would she run out of here screaming for help that madwomen had invaded her studio? "But all of it is true."

Claire wandered off to inspect the blocks of stone in various degrees of completion.

Abbie began by how they had rescued the girl from a burning house.

Pauline gasped, her hand at her throat, her gaze fixed on the child.

Margaret whispered their enemy had killed her parents.

Ruby added he was headed here. "Are you expecting anyone this morning?"

"Robert's cousin." Pauline released a put-upon sigh and turned to them, rolling her eyes. "He is to call this afternoon. Insisted it was beholden on him to support me during this trying time."

Abbie didn't like the sound of this. "Would that be Robert's cousin, Nevin?"

Pauline's brows knit. "Are you two acquainted?"

Despite her dislike of the man, Abbie shook her head. Technically, she'd never met him. "I've heard stories."

"My parents are expected tomorrow." Pauline twirled her chisel. "That will save me having to entertain him alone."

A soft knock sounded and then a young girl entered with a round tray with a teapot and cup. Her wide-eyed glance swept over Abbie and her family before she set the tray on the table beside her mistress.

"Thank you, Lucy. We'll need four more cups and more tea. Also, bring hot buttered rolls and scrambled eggs."

"Golly!" Claire ran over. "All that?"

Pauline's gaze seemed to feast on the child. Abbie suspected she was still deeply grieving the death of her daughter. "Once you fetch that, I am not to be disturbed."

"Yes, my lady." The servant curtsied and hurried out.

"Lucy!" Abbie raised her tone.

The maid swung around, mouth agape.

"Don't tell anyone we're here with your mistress."

The maid turned to Pauline. At her nod, Lucy gulped and left.

"Can she be trusted?" Ruby pulled up a chair.

"With my life." Pauline poured a cup and handed it to Abbie. "Now, I wish to hear how you know Robert." Her gaze speared her. "And why he would permit you to call him by his Christian name? By *that* name?" Her lips quivered. "I am the only other who calls him Robert."

Abbie's cheeks heated. Why had he not insisted she call him Matthew or my lord or Lord Ashford?

"The first time I met your husband," she chose her words with care, "he mentioned his name was Robert."

Her hostess gasped, eyes widening.

Abbie moved closer to her. "We've come from the future. Several hundred years, in fact. In my time, your husband is my closest and most trusted adviser."

Pauline gave a firm shake of her head, and stumbling off her chair, she backed away from all of them. "No. That cannot be. I do not believe you."

Abbie took a deep breath to calm her nerves because this conversation was pushing Pauline closer to the door. She was losing her. "Have you never had an otherworldly experience?"

She half expected this educated and gifted lady to say another emphatic, *No*, but Pauline hesitated and her gaze skittered away from Abbie.

"Tell me about it. We have little time to waste."

Pauline took a deep breath, crossing her arms as if to protect herself. "Once, a long time ago, shortly after I met a grieving Robert, and I was busy sculpting his brother's figure, I thought I sensed a man in a red uniform who kept pace by my side on my lonely treks along a beach each night. It felt as if he were guarding me. I do not know from what. I put it down to my overstimulated imagination. Even my maid, Lucy, insisted she never saw him."

Abbie listened to Pauline's tale, wondering if Robert's brother Geoffrey could have been visiting the woman his brother was falling in love with. Her instincts hummed a firm *yes* to that guess.

"I'd not sensed that spirit since my marriage." Pauline's wavering gaze met Abbie's, as if to check if her listener was about to mock her. "Until recently. He reappeared last night, while I was missing Robert."

Abbie latched on to their common experience. "That is how I met your husband in my time. He was a spirit in St. Michael's graveyard."

"Oh, no!" Pauline's hand covered her mouth, her eyes squinting, as if in pain. "That means he's not at rest. At peace. In Heaven." Her eyes filled with tears that overflowed.

Claire rushed over to Pauline and hugged her. "Don't cry. Abbie will watch over him."

Abbie focused on their current dilemma. "My lady, your husband sent us to you because Claire needs your help."

"To be this child's guardian?" The lady wiped her face with a handkerchief with one hand, while holding the child close with her other arm.

Another knock interrupted Abbie and her family's tense meeting with Pauline.

The door opened and Lucy rolled a tea trolley into her mistress's studio. It held breakfast dishes and a tea service. After a quick scan of the room, the maid studiously avoided eye contact with everyone. She served in silence, walking around the table to pour tea into each cup, and then hurried out.

Margaret and Ruby dragged more chairs to the table.

Abbie passed the rolls and scrambled eggs to the others.

Pauline urged Claire to take a seat and served her, but the child toyed with her food. Her wide-eyed gaze rested on the lady of the house, more than on her much-anticipated hot-buttered roll.

Pauline's gaze, too, strayed to Claire. Often.

For the fourth time, to Abbie's count. She tucked into her food with secret delight.

"Are all of you from the...the future?" Pauline tapped the table beside Claire's plate. "Eat."

A smile lit up Claire's face, and she took a big scoop of scrambled eggs.

"The three of us, yes, but not the child." At Pauline's openness to the possibility they were telling the truth, Abbie's estimation of her hostess rose even higher. "Which is why we cannot take her with us. She belongs here. It was your husband's most fervent wish that you not be alone or lost in your grief over him."

"Taking care of Claire could ally his concerns and ours," Margaret put in.

"When we arrived here and saved Claire," Abbie added, "we were left with a dilemma. How to keep this child safe? If her enemy learns Claire is alive, he will seek her out. She must go into hiding, while we must return home."

Ruby pulled out her hourglass from her cleavage. "I'd say in less than a few hours."

"So soon?" Pauline's voice rose in a note of panic. Then she stroked Claire's hair. "I can take her to my parents' home."

"No." Ruby shook her head. "You must both change your names. And best if you left England altogether."

Pauline snatched back her hand and held it close to her chest, staring at Ruby as if she'd grown a second head. "Where would we go? What about my family and friends, and my commissions? I cannot simply leave those I love with no explanation."

Harsh as Ruby had sounded, Abbie sided with her. "That is what you must do."

"Then my answer is, *No!*" Pauline's unyielding gaze collided with Abbie's. "What about Robert? He needs me now more than ever. I will not abandon him to face his fate alone."

Ruby's face set, as if she intended to insist that if Pauline refused to care for Claire, she would. Despite her mother's support for this idea, it was far too dangerous to leave an unpredictable Ruby behind. Abbie shook her head, unable to agree to that course of action.

The clatter of hoofs had them all swinging toward a narrow front window. Pauline went to that one, which overlooked the castle bailey. "It is Nevin. He is early."

Abbie and her family hurried after her, and Ruby shifted Pauline out of the way.

Peering over her mother's shoulder, Margaret gasped. "It's the Earl of Ashford!"

"What?" Abbie pushed them both aside to look out.

"That's not Robert." Pauline shot them a scathing glance. "Have any of you even met my husband? Has this all been a pack of cruel lies?"

Margaret moved closer to Pauline. "It's the earl from our time."

"That is impossible." Pauline shook her head and returned to her place at the work table. "Or are you asserting that Nevin can travel across time, too?"

That was a troubling thought, but a more plausible idea churned in Abbie's stomach like a writhing snake. What if the Earl of Ashford, from her time, *was* Nevin, Robert's cousin? Could Nevin be the Roman? The one who had killed her friends, hurt Figg, and who'd been killing Grimms for centuries? She returned to the work table and sank into her seat, pulse hammering, legs too shaky to hold her up.

"He did not travel back in time." Ruby's tone was firm as she took her seat.

"He didn't have to." Abbie's tone was grave. "He's been here all along."

"How can Robert's cousin be the same man you are familiar with?" Pauline tried to instill reasonableness into a world that had turned insane. "You intimated you are from the far future. No one lives that long."

"He uses spells to keep himself alive." Ruby rapped her fingers on the table. "The last time I saw him, he was disguised as a Chinese gentleman. After his injury, he appeared as a completely different man." Ruby caught and held Abbie's gaze. "Is Kiros a black man?"

Abbie nodded.

Ruby leaned back and heaved a heavy sigh. "Then more than a Roman medallion links the two of them."

Abbie took a deep breath to quell her turmoil. They had taken a giant step in identifying their enemy.

"Nevin looks much older now than when Robert met him a year ago." Pauline gently stroked Claire's hair. "My husband wondered if his cousin might be ailing."

"If he's so different, it could be because our enemy took over Nevin's life." Abbie shuddered at what he might have done to the real Nevin. "Robert's actual cousin likely lies in a grave somewhere, lost and forgotten."

"Oh, poor Nevin." Pauline covered her mouth with her hand. "I feel dreadful about all the horrid things I've thought about him this past year."

Ruby sat up, her eyes lighting as Pauline's dimmed. "His injury must have depleted his resources. He might have reached the end of his disguising days."

"Isn't glamor the simplest of spells?" Margaret queried.

Ruby shook her head. "He doesn't use simple glamor. Instead of displaying a new face, he becomes the person he's pretending to be, down to every cell of his body. That's why his disguises are so good. That requires a significant amount of magical use."

"Then that could also be why he's unable to control his appearance with precision to match the real Nevin." For the first time, Margaret appeared more intrigued than defeated. "Is he now stuck in this aging form he's taken on? Is that why he still looks the same in our time?"

# Chapter Nine

A knock sounded on the studio door before Lucy stuck her head inside. "My lady, you have a visitor. It's the master's cousin, and he insists on speaking to you. He's waiting in the great hall, per his wishes. What should I tell him?"

"Oh, no!" Claire flung herself onto Pauline. "You mustn't let him hurt you like he did Mama and Papa."

"Tell him her ladyship is at work and will be along shortly." Abbie's raised hand cut off Pauline. "Offer him tea. And Lucy."

"Yes, miss?"

"Don't mention that we're here with your mistress."

Lucy hesitated, glancing from her to the others crowding her mistress's studio. Finally, her gaze settled on Pauline, who nodded.

"Yes, my lady. As far as I know, you are here alone."

"Good girl." Pauline sent her a shaky smile, still cuddling Claire.

The door shut behind the maid, and her footsteps faded.

Abbie moved around the table to Pauline's side. "So far, you've accepted our outlandish words on faith, and on Robert's backing, my lady. I'm about to show you physical proof we are more than ordinary folk."

Pauline's gaze widened, and she stood to face Abbie, shoulders back, chin up.

After a quick scan of the table, Abbie picked up Pauline's chisel. "Hold this."

Raising her eyebrow, Pauline accepted her tool.

Abbie pointed her Left forefinger ring at Pauline. "Arthur,

extend your shield over this lady, and use the chisel as your touchpoint. Do it so she witnesses what you're building until it's completed."

The ring's energy flared and sparked as it met the sharp, metallic blade before the light swept across Pauline.

The lady sucked in her breath. "Oh, my! I have goosebumps all over."

"I told you my godfairies were magical." Claire clapped and twirled. "They'll protect you."

Arthur's shield faded from sight, as did the chisel, but her ring's connection to Pauline remained strong and comforting.

"That shield will keep you from harm as long as you hang on to that chisel. Do not let go of it. Do you understand?"

Pauline nodded.

Abbie breathed, her chest still tight at the idea of allowing this woman, a norm, to face a powerful mage alone. Robert wouldn't approve, but what choice did they have? "Find out what Nevin wants, and then send him packing. Use whatever excuses you must, but he cannot stay in this castle. Under no circumstance mention that you've spoken to us."

"Is she still in danger?" Claire's voice spiked as she huddled beside Pauline.

"I shall be fine." The lady stood, clutching her chisel in one hand and hugging the girl with her other arm.

"You mustn't go to heaven or become a spirit." Claire's earnest words proved she'd been following their discussion with roiling emotions.

Abbie's heart squeezed with sorrow for a child who was still in the throes of grieving her parents' loss.

"I am merely going to visit a cousin, love." Pauline's gaze

pleaded with Abbie for intervention.

Abbie gently tugged Claire away. "She'll be all right." Her pulse pounded in opposition to her reassuring words.

"Will you be here upon my return?" Pauline removed her apron, her fingers trembling as she undid the knot.

"We'll be here." Ruby came around and gave her a reassuring nod. "Don't tarry."

"Good luck." Margaret frowned as the door closed behind Pauline. "I don't like sending her off alone to meet that villain. What if he hurts her?"

"Oh, no!" Hugging Abbie tight, Claire wept.

"He won't." Abbie soothed the child, shooting her mother a warning glance. "He's merely here to comfort Pauline because the authorities have arrested her husband."

Claire had left her valise on the table. Abbie pointed to the case. For just a blink, the child had forgotten her last promise to her father–*guard the case.*

The child's face scrunched in horror at her mistake, and she raced to pick up her valise and hug it to her chest, before she hurried over to glance out the narrow window by the door.

Arthur reinstated his protection over Claire by reconnecting to the valise.

Abbie wished she could tell Claire that everything would be all right. Yet, she wasn't certain all would work out. "For such a little thing, she's been through a lot."

"Much has been taken from her." Margaret mirrored Abbie's whispering tone, but her gaze rested on Ruby, as if she were recalling her childhood growing up without a mother.

"Even more will be asked of her in the coming days, weeks, even years." Ruby spoke in a hard voice, her fists clenched.

"She'll have the entirety of Britain's Grimm family legacy to safeguard."

Abbie's gaze wandered back to Claire, standing on her toes, peering out the window. In the short time Claire had known Pauline, she seemed to have accepted the lady of this house in the light of a new caretaker. Someone she trusted to watch over her. That burgeoning relationship would help Claire after Abbie and her family left this timeline.

"Did you see the longing in Pauline's gaze after we introduced Claire?" Margaret's tone was layered with meaning.

"In Claire, she sees the daughter she lost." Ruby's softly spoken words were a statement of fact rather than speculation. As if she had no doubts about it.

Was that what happened to Ruby after she gave up her baby to another to raise? Had she seen her "Peggy" in every child she encountered? Abbie placed her arm around Ruby.

Her gran blinked rapidly and turned her head away, but she didn't withdraw from Abbie's hold. "To ensure Pauline stays safe, I could watch her while staying out of sight. Even if Nevin sees me, it won't matter. He recognized me as he left Claire's burning house. He already knows I'm in England, in this time, decades past when I should have died."

Abbie snatched her arm from around Ruby. "Safer for all if we stay out of sight."

"Abbie's correct." Margaret's soothing tone, if not her words, suggested she had sympathy for Ruby. "We must guard Claire."

Ruby paced the room. "I have a bad feeling about Pauline being alone with the man."

Since Nevin's arrival, Abbie's Grimm instincts, too, had

been screaming that trouble abounded. "Our prime concern has to be Claire's safety."

"Where is she?" Her mother's chair skidded as she stood.

Abbie swung around to where she'd last seen Claire. The child and her valise were missing. "Oh, no! I bet she's gone after Pauline. She's probably worried she'll lose her as she did her parents. I should have seen this coming."

Ruby rushed to the door, with Abbie's mother at her heels.

Abbie was right behind them, but she slammed her hand on the door to keep it shut.

"What now?" Ruby snapped.

"We need a plan. We can't rush out there. That's how Claire's parents ended up dead."

"Good thinking." Margaret leaned against the door and shut her eyes. "Do you have one? My mind's mush. I just want to throttle that man."

Abbie pictured the gruesome scene in Claire's home superimposed over this castle, and shivered. "Since Pauline's in the great hall, that's where Claire is likely headed. Can you sense her there, Mum?"

Margaret frowned. "She's somewhere in this castle, but I can't narrow it down, no. I'm too frazzled. Give me a moment."

"It's alright. I'll use Levi. But we shouldn't all go together. Let's separate and approach the great room from different directions."

"Good." Ruby checked around the studio. "That will give us the element of surprise, but we need weapons."

"I have one." Abbie raised her right arm where Hafgufa was sequestered.

Margaret hurried over to the work table and grabbed

Pauline's hammer.

Ruby reached for a nearby slender, but hefty piece of marble, wielding it like a cudgel. Mother and daughter were more alike than either realized.

"As long as you two hang on to your pumpkin and thimble," Abbie faced her family returning with their chosen weapons, "you'll have Arthur's protection. But this situation calls for something more. I'm going to use an artifact from Claire's valise."

"A little late for that, isn't it?" Dollops of scorn dripped off Ruby's words.

Abbie held out her hand. "Ruth, I need you." The hand mirror artifact settled on her palm.

"Nicely done!" Her mother flashed an approving smile.

"Can I do that, too?" Ruby held out her hand. "Wish bomb, come."

Abbie sensed a wish bomb in Claire's valise quiver. It was as if she were as intimately connected to Claire's artifacts now as she was with her items back home. They must have all awoken to her presence as Grimm Guardian. And that wish bomb was about to obey Ruby's call.

Abbie silently ordered the wish bomb to, *"Stay!"*

Ruby's palm remained empty.

Abbie's tense shoulders released their stiff stance. *"Good wish bomb."*

"This is better." Abbie held up the mermaid-handled mirror to distract Ruby. She twirled the handle until the mirror faced her mother. "Make my mother invisible to all but Ruby, Claire, Pauline, and myself."

Her mother remained visible beside her, but when Abbie

glanced in the mirror, Margaret's reflection was gone.

"Oooh!" Ruby gazed into the mirror, mouth agape. "I'd wondered how that artifact worked. Wait." Ruby frowned, turning back to Abbie. "Does this mean you could have taken the hourglass from me anytime you wanted?"

"You've come fully into your talent." Margaret's words carried a proud lilt. "As your powers grew, I sensed you'd one day become the most powerful Grimm."

"Then you should have trained her better!" Ruby snapped.

To stop another argument, Abbie pointed the mirror at Ruby. "Ruth, make Ruby invisible to all but my mother, Claire, Pauline, and myself. Do the same to me, making me only visible to Ruby, my mother, Claire, and Pauline."

Ruby gazed in the mirror. "That worked."

*"Return to Claire's case."* The mirror vanished.

Abbie opened the door. "Let's hope Pauline hangs onto that chisel, and Claire doesn't let go of her valise again. That will ensure Arthur's protection stays over them."

Her mother followed her outside and hurried toward the central courtyard with her hammer. She must plan to approach the great hall from the north.

Ruby rushed down the right corridor, so Abbie took the left. Since this castle was square in structure, they should be able to meet up again from various directions.

Abbie pulled out Levi. *"Locate Claire."*

She followed his instructions until Levi gave a confusing direction. *"Turn left."*

That direction was away from the great hall where Pauline was. Instead, this way would take her into the southeast turret. Had Claire gone up there? Why? Abbie took a deep, calming breath. For now, the why didn't matter. She entered the tower room, her Grimm instincts riding her steps. Skirts lifted, she flew up the stairs.

The higher she climbed, the slower her steps moved. On the top floor, heaving for each breath, her throat raw, and legs trembling, Abbie flung open the only door out in that top room.

Cool, fresh air bathed her.

Ahead, a boy led Claire away along the walkway of the castle's battlements. The girl still carried her valise. That meant she had allowed this stranger closer, even invited his touch, or Arthur's protection would have prevented the contact. What was the foolish girl thinking?

"Claire!" The word came out hoarse.

Claire turned back.

The boy pulled her along. "Come on! No one's there."

Of course, unlike Claire, he couldn't see Abbie.

He dragged Claire, but she pulled back.

Abbie ran toward Claire, stumbling a little on shaky legs. When she had a clear shot, she struck out her cord to snag the girl around the waist.

With a cry, the boy let go of Claire and raced away empty-handed.

Relief washed over Abbie in a cool wave, fresher than a beach-side breeze. Using her cord, she drew Claire closer and then took her hand. "Who was that?"

"He was taking me to Lady Ashford to save her. Did he lie about that?"

"Why would she be up here?"

Claire shook her head, a tear slipping down her cheek.

Abbie retracted her cord and held the girl close. "Claire, not everyone tells the truth."

Claire might be gullible, but why had the boy brought her up to the battlements? Had he intended to throw Claire off the parapet?

If so, Abbie trembled at the child's close call. "Come on. I'm taking you back to the studio."

"No!" Claire pulled out of Abbie's hold. "I want to make sure Lady Ashford's safe. Please, will you help me check on her, Godfairy Abbie?"

A *whoosh* at her back had Abbie swinging around. Above, a hot-air balloon swung around the northern tower. It had three balloons strapped side-by-side above an elongated, elaborate basket. She gaped at the flying balloons. Did they have such things during the Regency?

The boy who'd been leading Claire climbed onto the parapet and dove toward the basket. He missed and fell.

Abbie's heart sank.

Miraculously, the boy caught a rope hanging off the side of the basket and hung on, swinging in midair. Then the aeronaut pulled the dangling boy aboard.

Abbie gulped in a much-needed breath.

"Oh!" Claire's gaze was glued to the flying basket. "Is that thing magic, too, Godfairy Abbie?"

"I don't know."

The airborne contraption adjusted its direction and headed straight for them. That thing could steer! Before the invention of a propulsion system?

Abbie gulped. Someone wielding magic must control it. Grabbing Claire's hand, she raced for the tower door. "Run! Or we won't be able to help Lady Ashford at all."

Without argument, the child sprinted beside Abbie.

Once inside the tower room, Abbie barred the door and, with Claire's permission, took out Ruth from her valise. She ordered Ruth to make Claire invisible. Then, dropping the mirror into Claire's case, they headed downstairs.

If Nevin knew to send these strangers to snatch Claire here, he was aware Pauline was helping the child. So, he meant Pauline no good. Now, Abbie wanted to find the lady of the house as badly as Claire did.

On the ground floor, heaving for breath, she took out Levi to locate Pauline's location. Abbie and Claire followed the compass's lead. Levi took them directly toward the great hall, where servants crowded the closed door leading to it.

They shushed each other and pressed their ears to the wood. Even the butler was nearby, pacing. It was as if he were working himself up to disobeying orders. Pauline must have asked him to stay outside.

What Abbie needed was for everyone to move aside so she and Claire could enter that room. She tiptoed behind a maid and, picking up a clay ornament from a side table, threw it as far as she could. It crashed with a loud clamor and pieces scattered. Everyone dispersed, some toward the crash, others fleeing the scene.

Abbie eased the door open, and the two entered, shutting the door behind them.

Inside the great room, a gentleman spoke to Pauline. He sat with his back to them. Tall, gray-haired, and impeccably dressed, his posture was as arrogant as the day ten-year-old Abbie had been brought in front of him to apologize for vandalizing his property, Robert's gravestone.

Abbie shook off her past. With Claire's trembling hand in her grip, she placed a finger to her lips.

The child nodded, lips quivering.

They tiptoed to the side of the room.

To Pauline's credit, she did not bat an eyelash at Abbie and Claire's impromptu entrance. So far, she appeared safe and unharmed, with servants nearby to rush in here if their mistress called out.

"I am sorry, Nevin." Pauline set her teacup on the table and stood. On the table beside the tea tray was her chisel.

Abbie's heart lodged in her throat. How could Pauline have set down that tool?

"I am in no fit state to entertain guests today." Pauline pointed to the door. "You'd better leave and visit another day."

Nevin jumped to his feet, jaw hardened and eyes narrowed. He appeared anything but willing to comply with her reasonable-sounding request.

Pauline's back stiffened and her gaze fell on her chisel. "I am retiring for the night." She reached for her tool. "I shall expect you to be gone before I return downstairs in the morning."

Quick as a fox, his hand snaked out and grabbed her upper arm before the lady had picked up the chisel. "Not so fast, my lady."

"How dare you place your hand on me, sir." Pauline's tone dripped ice. "Release me!"

"Or what?" His sneer lined every wrinkle and layered his furious tone. "Your holier-than-thou husband's not here to defend you."

"My servants are." She opened her mouth.

He slammed a hand over her lips. "I would not do that, my lady. Not unless you want your servants as dead as your child was, once I needed her gone. To my surprise, hurting your husband with that killing wasn't satisfying enough. So, his demise is next on my list."

Pauline blanched at each vindictive word Nevin uttered while Abbie stood frozen. Nevin had killed Lizzie? Why? To hurt Robert? Again, why?

The answer rang out clear as a bell. What was Nevin's goal? Release demons into the Earth. Robert's injury happened in Spain when he stopped a demon uprising. He must have unwittingly spoiled Nevin's plan to release those demons.

"Leave my mama be!" Claire cried out, drawing Abbie back into this perilous moment. Pulling away from Abbie's nerveless hold, the girl dropped her valise and ran toward Pauline, arms extended.

Abbie shuddered. In dropping that valise, she'd broken Arthur's protection over her, leaving herself open to being attacked. And the case, once Claire let go of it, became visible.

Nevin swung around. "Who said that? Who is in here?"

"*I am too stretched.*" Arthur confirmed Abbie's worst fear. "*I cannot form a new connection to the child.*"

Ignoring the valise, Abbie ran to protect the child with her shield. Capturing her, she held her in place, though Claire struggled to get away, kicking and punching.

"Ah, the Grimm child must be here." Nevin's syrupy voice ground against Abbie's last working nerve. "You've made yourself invisible. But how thoughtful to bring me a present. I sense great power in that valise."

"Oh, no!" Claire stopped struggling, and glanced at back her valise. "I'm supposed to guard that."

Oddly, Nevin didn't sprint to grab the case, but stood perfectly still, shifting his hold on Pauline to free a hand, even as that lady struggled to release herself. His gaze was fixed on the case.

*Ah!* If the case moved, he'd know where and when to strike. His curled right hand glowed from within.

Abbie's internal alarm bells reverberated, deafening her. Ignoring her internal Grimm call to action, she stayed put, holding onto Claire. She watched Nevin watching the case and readied her cord to spring out. She waited for a chance to attack him without endangering Pauline or Claire.

# Chapter Ten

A door at the side banged open, and Ruby strode into the great room. She shut the door on servants peering in and brandished her marble cudgel. "Well, well, well. So, we meet again. Nevin, is it now? How have you been since our last encounter?" She tilted her head and studied him from head to boots. "You look a tad older. Mortality creeping up on you?"

Still clutching Pauline, Nevin swung around to face Ruby, and then he stiffened. "You!"

Ruby had wished for the mirror to end its invisibility spell. She was here to draw his attention from Abbie, Claire, Pauline, and the valise that contained the entire Grimm family's magical legacy.

Heat suffused Abbie's heart at this wonderful, foolish, brave woman's bold action, but the repercussion of this open confrontation sent shivers up her spine.

Nevin flung a magical lightning spear straight at Ruby. She cringed aside, but Arthur's shield bounced the strike, and it hit a painting on the wall. The frame toppled and crashed to the floor with a startling *bang*.

Nevin snarled, and Ruby smirked.

Claire stomped on Abbie's foot. Tears streaming down her face, the child tore out of Abbie's loosened grip and raced for her valise, her steps pounding toward her precious case.

Pauline took that moment of distraction to grab her chisel and plunge it into Nevin's hand gripping her upper arm. "That's for hurting Lizzie!"

Nevin screamed, his face contorting as he plucked the

chisel out of his hand.

Released, Pauline raced past Abbie, her determined gaze fixed on Claire. She flew to tackle the child who had arrived at the bag.

Nevin fired a lightning bolt at Pauline, left-handed.

Abbie leapt to intercept that strike. His magical fire hit her left side, the force spinning her. She landed on the carpet and rolled. The lightning bolt had bounced off Arthur's shield and slammed into the mantle, sending shards of bricks flying.

The blow would have blasted Pauline or Claire if it had reached them. Abbie shuddered at their close call. Scrambling to her feet, she shot out her cord toward Nevin and snagged him by his ankle.

With a sharp crack, glass shattered, and a hammer flew into the room. The weapon whacked Nevin across the side of his forehead. He swayed, dropping to his knees, and groaned.

"Got him!" Margaret peered in from the north garden through the broken window, fists raised and pumping.

"Cracking!" Ruby ran to Nevin with her cudgel and hammered at him.

Fending off her attack, he shouted, "FIGG!"

A horrendous growl and ferocious barks came from outside. Abbie swung toward the broken window. Figg burst into the great hall past where Abbie's mother had been standing. *Please, Lord, let her be okay.*

The black and white mutt landed on four giant clawed paws, his nails rasping against the stone floor as he transformed into a slobbering beast five times his size.

"Kill them all!" Nevin shoved Ruby away from him with force.

Abbie re-directed her cord from Nevin to Figg and ensnared the dog mid-leap around his expanded chest.

Nevin was headed for the door, bent over his bleeding hand and supporting his bruised head.

She drew a breath to warn about him escaping, but Figg landed on top of her, sending her toppling. Her breath whooshed out. Arthur's protection kept the dog's fangs and claws from harming her, but she still struggled to subdue the ferocious beast. He was heavy and his hot breath pungent. His eyes, full of a killing frenzy, sent her pulse thudding.

Thank heavens for Arthur's protection or she'd be dead. Abbie heaved the dog aside, but kept hold of him with her cord to prevent him going after Pauline or Claire.

Ruby scrambled from where she'd landed and raced after Nevin, who'd reached the side door through which her gran had entered.

He turned and sent another spear of magic that scorched a sofa and spun it toward Ruby. The villain then opened the door and shoved past servants gathered outside.

Tied to the dog, Abbie couldn't stop him.

Ruby, who had safely avoided that flaming furniture soaring toward her, went after Nevin.

"Leave him, Ruby!" The door slammed shut behind her gran. Big surprise. Where was Margaret? Abbie couldn't lose both of them.

"She's not listening." Abbie's mother heaved open the broken window and climbed into the great room. "Since you have the dog in hand, I'll check on Pauline and Claire."

Her mother's decision to abandon Ruby to Nevin had Abbie wanting to shake both stubborn women, but she had her hands full dealing with Figg, who jumped on her again. She stiffened her cord and used its magic to shove Figg off her and keep him at arm's length.

He snarled and fought his confinement.

"Figg, settle down!" Abbie snapped.

The dog stopped and gave her a startled glance.

Taking advantage of his surprise, she stood. "Sit!"

Figg shook his head, as if flicking away an annoying fly, sending spittle flinging in all directions. Then he barked with ferocity and twisted to bite at the cord confining him.

A familiar vibration thrummed in Abbie's bones. Someone was casting a spell. Nevin? She sensed it coming from outside. Worried for Ruby's safety, Abbie hurried to the broken window, dragging Figg along behind her.

Outside in the courtyard, Nevin's carriage sped toward the drawbridge. Servants had gathered on the drive to watch the spectacle. Ruby was there, placing something on the gravel. Too far to see what, but what else would it be but her pumpkin artifact? The spell Abbie had sensed being triggered must be Basil, and invoked in plain sight of non-magical folk.

*"Basil, don't change!"* Abbie held out her left hand. *"Pumpkin, hourglass, to me. Now!"*

Both artifacts appeared on her palm. The hourglass held precious little sand still to fall.

Ruby's scream added to Figg's riotous barks.

Abbie ignored them both. *"Hourglass, how long do we have left?"*

*"An hour and fifty-seven minutes."*

Her stomach fluttered at the fast-diminishing stretch to set all to right. She focused on the two artifacts. *"You're both to stay put unless I say otherwise.*" She then stuffed them into the reticule hanging off her wrist.

"Abbie." Her mother's voice broke on her name. "Lady Ashford's hurt. She needs you."

What? How could that be? No time to sort that out. She had to neutralize Figg before the servants entered to care for their mistress. "Hafgufa, can you calm this dog?"

"*Sleep,*" Hafgufa murmured.

The dog slumped to the floor and lay still, and the sound level dropped from hellish to peaceful. Abbie released a sigh. "How long will he be like that?"

"*He will awake in a couple of hours, or if I wake him.*"

Using her magical cord's assist, she dragged Figg behind a large chair in the corner of the room, covered him with a throw, and used Ruth to turn him invisible for good measure. Then she ended the invisibility spell over the rest of them before returning the mirror to Claire's valise.

"Abbie, hurry!" Her mother glanced over.

"Arthur, what happened to Lady Ashford?" Abbie raced toward Pauline. "Your protection over me should have prevented Nevin's strike from reaching her."

"*Most of it was deflected, but a portion went beneath you when you dove. That might have struck Lady Ashford.*"

The mantle had shattered when Nevin's fire struck it. If even a sliver of his magic had touched Pauline, what would that have done to her? She could not die. That would change this timeline, leave Robert devastated, and hurt a brave woman who had valiantly tried to save Claire.

Pulse thundering, hands clammy, Abbie knelt by her mother's side to examine Pauline. The poor woman lay utterly still. Her right side looked burned; the gown singed from shoulder to waist.

Claire wailed beside them, and Margaret pulled her aside to give Abbie room and peace to work.

She checked Pauline's pulse. A fast *thud-thud* beat against her fingers and Abbie's breath *whooshed* out. Pauline may be unconscious, but she wasn't dead.

Abbie checked her patient, head to foot. Aside from the burns, she had a bent rib, distending her clothing. Likely caused by her fall. Pauline moaned and Abbie winced at the pain she must be in. Thankfully, because Arthur's shield had blunted Nevin's lightning shot, it had only grazed her, leaving behind first-degree burns. Painful, but healable.

A loud rapping sounded.

Clutching Claire, her mother glanced over at the door. "It's probably servants. Shall I let them in?"

Abbie nodded.

"Come in!" Margaret called out.

The door flung open, and the butler rushed in. One look at his injured mistress and he let out a keening howl. "What's happened to Lady Ashford?"

Several servants crept into the room behind him. One of them was Lucy. Good girl!

"Your mistress is injured." Abbie focused on Lucy. This young maid would have to care for Pauline after Abbie and her family left this timeline. Was she up to the task? "She's received burns and has a broken rib."

"I...um... I should send for a physician." The butler's sputtered words sounded more like a question.

Abbie needed his cooperation, too. "I need your

assistance."

"Yes, miss." Eyes wide, hands clasped, he held her glance, as if begging for instructions. "Anything you need."

"Fetch bandages, warm water, and whiskey."

He sent servants scurrying in different directions to procure all Abbie requested.

Ice to cool the burns would be helpful, but there were no refrigerators yet. What had Robert mentioned about ice cream? He'd called them ices, kept cool in icehouses.

She grabbed the butler's arm. "Is there an icehouse nearby?"

"Yes, miss. Within the castle premises."

"Brilliant. Bring chopped pieces of ice to cool Lady Ashford's burns. Now, we must carry her to her chamber. Use the chaise over there to lift her so she is less likely to be jarred while being carried upstairs."

He called over a few footmen.

Pauline moaned. "Claire–"

"She's safe." Abbie gentled her tone. "You saved her, but you're hurt. We're going to take care of you."

Pauline clutched Abbie's arm and then cried out.

"Don't move!"

"You were right." Pauline's voice trembled. "I should have listened. We must safeguard Claire. From Nevin."

"I'll arrange all the details." Abbie kept her voice firm to calm Pauline's fears. "Now, lie still." She nodded to the butler.

At his gesture, servants carried their injured mistress out of the room on the chaise.

Abbie rose to her feet, bones aching, shoulders heavy.

Claire clutched at Abbie. "Please help her!"

"I will." Abbie hugged Claire, and kissed her head. "Trust me to take care of Lady Ashford. I can make her better."

Margaret pulled the child back, soothing her. Over the girl's head, she tapped her wrist.

Abbie nodded. They were running out of time, but now Pauline was willing to help Claire. That was a tremendous boon, though her being hurt would make travel difficult.

Abbie led the butler toward the open door. "Listen carefully. Your mistress is in imminent danger."

"I've sent for the physician." He glanced at the room behind them where the sofa smoked, chairs were toppled, and glass and broken mantle littered the floor. "Should we fetch the sheriff?"

Abbie shook her head. "Your master's cousin is responsible for the trouble your master and his wife now face."

"I knew no good would come from his visit." The man raised his arms, fists clenched. "I should never have allowed the mistress to meet him alone."

"He still means her harm. We must get her to safety."

"How? Where?" His voice trembled, hands wide open in a gesture of bewilderment.

"Your mistress must leave this castle. Today."

"The master will–"

Abbie took his hand, holding his gaze. "You will soon hear dire news. Stay strong. The staff will need to find other placements. They should take their belongings and leave this castle. By tonight, if possible. It will not be safe once that gentleman returns. And he will. Do you understand?"

The butler gulped, eyes wide, and then he nodded. "We will do as you say, miss. What about the mistress?"

"Once we've tended to her injuries, she must be spirited away in secret. Also, send word to your mistress's parents to not come here. That their daughter will contact them in due course. How soon can you have her ladyship's carriage ready?"

"We must bring the horses back from the pasture and prepare the vehicle for the journey. That will take time."

"Get started then. Hurry."

Once he rushed away, her plans churned.

Her mother inched closer. "What are you thinking?"

"I can use Ruth to make the carriage and horses invisible to get it past Nevin. Claire would have to take that spell off once they reach safety. But where could they go?"

"Speak to Pauline about that." Margaret led the girl away. "I'll explain to Claire how to use Ruth to do that."

"Thank you, Mum." Abbie turned to Lucy. She needed help to tend to Pauline and get her in a fit state to travel, but the maid was missing. Abbie huffed a sigh. She'd have to do this alone then.

She asked a servant for directions to Pauline's chamber and then climbed the stairs to the next floor. Her mind quieted, as if she'd put on a fresh EMT uniform to ready for a double shift.

Upstairs, in Pauline's bedchamber, the lady had fallen unconscious again. A small mercy. It took a few moments for Abbie to manipulate that one broken rib into its proper position. She prayed the break hadn't caused too much internal damage or harmed Pauline's lungs. No sign of blood pooling under her skin and her breaths were steady. Excellent signs.

Servants brought in water and bandages. Lucy rushed in behind them, her arms full of items. "I went to the stillroom for herbal remedies. The mistress mixes and stores them there."

She handed Abbie an ointment.

Abbie sniffed it. "Something sweet?"

"It's honey and bran, miss, for soothing burns. And this one is a lotion of wine and myrrh for healing wounds. My mother swears by that one." She then placed a pot on the side table that contained an aloe vera plant with long, succulent limbs. "The mistress procured that plant from a monastery up north after a visit. She said they'd been using such plants for centuries to tend to various illnesses."

The girl had brought exactly what Abbie needed to help Pauline. Fighting tears, Abbie hugged her. "You're a godsend. Aloe is excellent for helping heal burns."

Together, Abbie and Lucy washed and dressed Pauline's injuries. Abbie taught the maid how to repeat this routine in the coming days, especially using the insides of the aloe plant on the burns.

"Will you not be staying to care for the mistress, miss?" Lucy's voice trembled.

"I'm sorry, Lucy, but my family and I must leave soon. You must be brave and take care of Lady Ashford."

Lucy nodded, her eyes wide, showing the whites.

Pauline awoke and screamed.

Lucy sobbed quietly into her apron.

Abbie offered their patient a tincture of laudanum. "Lady Ashford, where can we take Claire?"

"To my Aunt Josephine's townhome in London." Pauline's words were a whisper. "We should be safe there. She knows how to keep a secret."

It would have to do. Soon, Pauline drifted off.

"Should we bandage her up tight, miss?" Lucy asked. "To

hold that rib in place?"

"No. I've straightened it as much as I can. All we can do now is leave it to settle into place. We don't want to constrict her ribs or she won't be able to breathe with ease. Her chest must expand and contract with no constriction."

"Oh, miss, I hadn't considered that."

Abbie washed her hands, holding the maid's gaze. "Lucy, your mistress will be in much pain for the next four to six weeks. Give her a bit of laudanum, but not too much or too often. Wean her off it as soon as you can. Cool the wounds with ice, often, and use the aloe vera plant to speed her healing. That and rest will do her wonders. Would you like me to write out these instructions?"

"No, I'll remember, miss. I've treated such wounds before. But thank heavens you were here."

This explained how this wonderful maid knew what medicines to fetch. Releasing a grateful sigh for the blessing that was Lucy, Abbie held out her arms.

Lucy ran to her.

"Lucy, Lady Ashford is going to heal. And she will sculpt again. But she can't do any of that while she's here."

The girl pulled away to gaze at Abbie with a frown. "Is that why we're taking her to Lady Josephine's?"

"Yes. But even there, you must be careful. The man who hurt your mistress, Lord Ashford's cousin, is sure to come looking for her."

"The master will protect her."

"He has been arrested, Lucy. His cousin is powerful and crafty. We must hide your mistress. Your job will not only be to tend to your mistress, but to ensure she remains out of sight, so he never finds her."

The maid gulped, raising her hands to cover her mouth.

"Lucy, you'll be leaving your family behind, and may not contact them for some time. Lady Ashford must have someone with her she trusts. Can you be that person?"

"Oh, yes, miss." Lucy firmed her shoulders. "To protect my lady, I will do anything she requires."

Abbie chuckled. "I cannot imagine a better companion for her. Now hurry and get ready. Pack a bag for your mistress. Only the essentials. You have little time. Go!"

Lucy started and then she ran around the room collecting things.

"Pack all the medicines you can," Abbie called out. "I'm uncertain how long it will take to gather the same supplies at your next destination."

Abbie headed back downstairs, her back stiff with tension, and a headache pounding at her temple. They were about to leave and Nevin was hurt, yes, but bound to return for Claire and her valise of valuable Grimm artifacts.

If Nevin found Pauline and Claire, would Abbie and her family even have a future to return to?

She checked the hourglass. *How much time left?*

*"Sixty-three minutes."*

If she and her family didn't leave by then, she'd never see her kids or Callum again. Heart pounding, Abbie's steps sped down the stairs.

The butler was pacing at the bottom landing.

Abbie stopped on the ground floor to face him, straightening her sagging shoulders. "Lady Ashford's wounds have been tended to. She's resting. Lucy is watching over her."

"Oh, thank you for that, miss." Relief washed over his face. "The horses have been gathered, and the carriage is being readied, but a gentleman and a boy have arrived. They are with the other two ladies and the young girl in the great room."

That surprised Abbie, considering the mess they'd left in that room, but her pulse jerked at the description of the visitors. A man and boy? The only two such people she'd seen in this time were ones from that hot-air balloon who'd tried to snatch Claire.

"Once the carriage is ready, come for me. And it must be within the hour. Understand?"

The butler nodded and checked his watch fob.

Abbie entered the great hall to find tea laid out on the freshly righted center table. Her mother and Ruby sat on the scorched sofa. Their two unexpected guests were on two plush chairs, facing the disheveled women.

Figg lay asleep behind them, his covering lost. At least he was still invisible. Small mercies.

On spotting her, man and boy, impeccably dressed and well-groomed, stood like perfect gentlemen.

If she hadn't witnessed this lad racing over the battlements and being hauled up by a rope into the hot-air balloon by that aeronaut, she might have taken them to be an ordinary pair of curious travelers coming to pay a visit to this castle.

# Chapter Eleven

On spotting Abbie entering the great room, Claire ran over with her valise. "Is Lady Ashford well?"

"She's resting." Abbie brushed stray hairs from the child's face. "She will recover, Claire. I'm certain of it."

"Oh, good." Claire hugged her tight. "Godfairy Margaret says Lady Ashford saved my life."

"She did, indeed." Abbie strolled with the child to her family's side.

Ruby glanced up at her, eyes cold, mouth a thin line of disapproval. She hadn't forgiven Abbie for stealing her hourglass and pumpkin yet. They had bigger problems to worry about. Namely, their unexpected guests.

Abbie's mother was seated beside Ruby, which was shocking, until she spotted Margaret's fierce grip on Ruby's hand. Ah, that's why Ruby hasn't jumped up to strangle Abbie.

She took her place beside her mother, wrinkling her nose at the smoky scent emanating from her darkened sofa seat. Claire squeezed in between her and Margaret. Taking their cue, the two male guests sat as well. They all pretended they weren't having tea on half-burned and tattered pieces of furniture, still smoking in places.

Her mother met her gaze and gave a knowing nod. "Abbie, this is Mr. Sacha Dubois, and his son Aubin." Mr. Dubois was in his early thirties with a memorable, chiseled face. The boy could be eleven, putting him about five years older than Claire. "They're from France."

The war was over, so a Frenchman might have traveled to

England without being apprehended by the army. Still, unusual to see French citizens in England so soon after the war. Worth checking on them.

She moved her hand behind her back to shield her action from their guests and called to Ruth. The mirror settled into her palm. She mind spoke. *"Ruth, can you tell when someone is wearing a disguise? Or is using glamor?"*

*"Oh, yes."*

*"Then tell me about the man and boy in this room."*

Claire squirmed to peer behind Abbie's back. "Is that mine or yours?"

Margaret tapped the child's knee. "Shhh!"

Claire swung around and checked inside her valise.

Ruth set off a vibration in Abbie's palm. Then the mirror went still. *"They are who they appear to be."*

*"Thank you, Ruth."* Abbie sent the mirror back.

Claire gasped and then shut her valise.

Abbie brought her arm forward and clasped her hands on her lap. "Why have you come here, Mr. Dubois?"

"Jacob and Wilhelm Grimm sent us." He had a strong French accent. "They have the sight for *activité magique.*"

Shock waves spun up Abbie's spine at this news.

"The brothers Grimm received a distress call from one of their male British relatives this past week." His narrowed gaze trained on Claire. "The message the runner carried said the enemy of all Grimms was after him and his wife and child. After looking into the matter, the brothers sent my son and I to investigate. Sadly, we arrived too late. The home we were directed to contained naught but ashes and unsightly remains. We identified the two we sought, but not the child."

Levi had said Claire's nearest relatives were in France. If what this man said about Claire's father was true, then this was confirmation that he had been the Grimm in that family. That Claire might be the first female Grimm in Abbie's family line. Was that why fate had directed them to this time?

"Seems coincidental." Ruby glared at their visitors. "Them coming here now."

Unlike Ruby, Abbie's qualms quieted about these two visitors. But, over and above what Ruth had revealed, it wouldn't hurt to verify that Mr. Dubois could be trusted. She sent her cord out in a thin golden thread down the back of her skirt and across the charred carpet to wrap around Mr. Dubois's ankle. He didn't flinch.

*"Hafgufa, is he telling the truth?"*

*"Yes."*

Claire leant toward her and spoke in the barest of whispers. "Good, because I like them."

Abbie retracted her cord, her lips tilting up. Claire's cheerful participation suggested she'd recovered from her earlier upset about Pauline. She had the makings of a great Grimm. Quick on her feet, shrewd, and possessing a generous heart. She squeezed the child's hand and winked at her. Abbie had one lingering question. "How did you know to come to this home to seek your target?"

"We spotted your flying carriage early this morning, *mademoiselle.* At first, we worried you were stealing the Grimm child for the enemy, since he was headed here as well. So, I sent Aubin to fetch the girl, but you intercepted him."

"How did you know that man was your villain?" Ruby snapped out the question. "He uses disguises."

"Mr. Jacob Grimm warned us to be wary of Lord Ashford's cousin." Mr. Dubois gave an eloquent shrug. "He has a way of tracking the enemy, whatever his guise. Once you fought him off, we decided we were on the same side."

"Are you truly godfairies?" His son Aubin spoke for the first time. His eyes were wide as he pointed at Claire. "She said that is what you all are."

"I would be interested in that answer as well." Mr. Dubois flashed a slight smile, his striking gray gaze resting on Ruby with interest.

"Aubin doesn't believe me." Claire turned to Abbie, her gaze upturned and full of hope. "Will you do magic for them?"

"We cannot cast spells." Technically true. Abbie straightened her gown, her mind grappling with how she could use these two to help Pauline and Claire escape Nevin's reach.

Ignoring Abbie and her mother, Mr. Dubois's gaze stayed rooted on Ruby, like a fox that had spotted a juicy vole. "How, then, did you make your carriage fly?"

"Do you have any proof the French Grimms sent you?" Ruby countered, crossing her arms.

Abbie barely followed the conversation. These two had a hot-air balloon. Could they follow Pauline's carriage by air to ensure she and Claire stayed safe? Could that balloon be maneuvered that precisely? Seemed unlikely, but she'd seen him swing it over the battlements with ease.

"Like your flying carriage, we, too, have an *artefact magique*." Mr. Dubois' voice quickened in pace and he sat up. "Our *montgolfière* should be proof enough of our Grimm connection."

Ruby shook her head, her tone turning scornful. "Are you

claiming you've been using a Grimm artifact?"

"*Oui, madam.* The first known crossing of a human-manufactured *montgolfière* involved travelers tossing everything overboard, including their clothing, to stay afloat. Then that balloon wandered at the will of the wind." He gestured to himself and his son. "We traveled from France within a day, as planned, and arrived fully clothed."

"Neither of you are Grimms." Ruby's tone was clipped and definitive. "You couldn't have operated a Grimm artifact."

"We are mere humans, *c'est vrai*, but we control this *montgolfière magique.* The Grimms gifted it to us to carry out this mission."

Ruby glared at him as if he were a squirming, slimy specimen she'd picked up out of a marsh. "They gave such a powerful artifact to a mortal?" She released a bark of laughter. "And approved your use of it? Why would they do such a foolish thing?"

That question spoke more to Ruby's lack of experience with gifting a Grimm artifact to a human, than of their guests' dishonesty. Abbie had temporarily gifted Levi to Callum, and he'd been able to use it.

"They must trust him." Abbie's mother reached past Claire and took Abbie's hand. She tilted her head toward Mr. Dubois and wriggled her eyebrows.

Frowning at her, Abbie studied him with care. His pupils were dilated as he stared at Ruby, and he wasn't breathing. But it wasn't in an affront to Ruby's attacks. This was a man captivated by her. If that tell on his face was accurate, and he had romantic hopes of a relationship with Ruby, they would soon be dashed.

Still, this was not her immediate concern. If the French Grimms had sent Mr. Dubois and his son here, at Claire's father's request no less, and in a *magical* hot-air balloon, then they were her best option for safeguarding Claire and Pauline.

A soft knock interrupted them.

"Come in." Abbie turned to the door.

The butler entered. "The balloon basket that landed and moored in the castle's south courtyard is lifting."

"*Quoi?*" Mr. Dubois jumped to his feet. "*Excusez-moi.* We must ensure the *montgolfière* is properly secured."

The moment all the males rushed out of the room, and the door shut, her mother turned to Abbie. "Are you thinking what I'm thinking?"

Abbie held her mother's gaze over Claire's head. "Traveling by hot-air balloon would be far more comfortable for my injured patient and much harder for Nevin to track."

"Are you two mad?" Ruby sprang to her feet to face them. "We know nothing about this Frenchman. How can you place Claire's well-being and our entire future in these strangers' hands?"

Margaret tapped her chin. "I think that hot-air balloon could easily carry Claire and Lady Ashford."

"Claire needs me!" Ruby's words burst out.

The girl gripped Abbie's hand. "Yes, I do."

Abbie's heart squeezed tight, and she patted their clasped hands. This was why she hadn't wanted Ruby to make promises about staying. Promises she couldn't keep.

She met Ruby's piercing gaze, keeping hers firm. "Claire will have Lady Ashford to watch over her and the Grimm brothers to guide her in the ways of her legacy."

"Men?" Ruby scoffed. "Have you forgotten what happened to your mother when a man brought her up? He turned her into a mindless killing machine. It's no wonder she left that life the first chance she had."

Margaret sucked in her breath.

"I won't allow that to happen to Claire." Ruby slashed her hand, her tone unequivocal. "Ours is a female Grimm line. Claire and her artifacts are part of our birthright. They both need to be protected. I should stay. The seashell artifact said as much."

That had been her question? If so, the seashell's answer was troubling. Especially since Abbie had yet to say to Pauline what the seashell had suggested she should.

Claire glanced from Ruby to Abbie, her mouth open.

Abbie shook her head. "The French Grimms have their own artifacts. They don't need Claire's. They'll be safe with her."

"It isn't just the artifacts." Ruby inched closer to Abbie. "Jacob and Wilhelm might be Grimms, but they're Frenchmen. Eventually, Claire must return to England. This is our territory to guard. She will need my guidance then."

"I agree with Ruby." Abbie's mother's words acted like a switch that turned off boiling water.

The fight in Abbie quieted, leaving her deflated.

"She should accompany Lady Ashford and Claire." Her mother tapped her chest. "I feel certain of that here."

Abbie studied the two women, and her certainty that Ruby could not stay faltered. Saying her mother was wrong would be like arguing that she should ignore her own Grimm instincts. She couldn't do it.

Margaret's gaze gentled as it held Abbie's. "This will allow her to be the mother she couldn't be to me."

Claire ran to hug Ruby. "I want Godfairy Ruby to come with me."

The fight abandoned Abbie. Her heart had never been in it, anyway. She didn't want to leave Claire without one of them to watch over her, teach her, and keep her safe. To love her. Was she going to allow this?

Goddess Kali would never approve. Abbie shuddered at all the Karma that might be affected if Ruby were left to run amok in this time. Yet, Abbie's lips pressed tight, obstructing her words of objection to this wild, uncharted course of action.

The door opened, and Mr. Dubois and his son returned. "The wind had loosened a mooring peg. All is well now."

The two Dubois took their seats, as did Ruby and Claire. This time, the child squeezed herself between Ruby and Margaret.

Abbie addressed the matter at hand. "How many can your balloon carry, sir?"

"How many did you have in mind?" His eyes narrowed, as if he were mentally calculating the area available within his basket. "I count the need for one more." His gaze rested on Claire.

"Three more." Sitting up straight and proud, Ruby turned to their French guests. "I'll be coming, too, along with Lady Ashford."

Mr. Dubois's frown transformed into a radiant smile. "You would be most welcome, *madam*. My basket can carry as many as needed. I can expand it."

Abbie turned to her guests. "You will have five extra

passengers."

"Five?" Margaret and Ruby spoke in unison.

"Lady Ashford, her maid, Claire, Ruby, and Figg." Abbie glanced at the sleeping dog.

"Who is this Figg?" Mr. Dubois frowned, following Abbie's gaze to the empty spot on the floor behind his chair.

*"Ruth."* Abbie focused on the hand mirror inside Claire's valise. *"Take the spell off Figg."*

The dog became visible.

*"Mon Dieu!"* Mr. Dubois jumped to his feet. "I am not taking that *monstre* into my basket."

Ruby snorted. "I can't believe you haven't killed that creature yet. If you're too squeamish, I'll do it."

"No!" Claire skirted the coffee table and ran to Figg's side. She huddled beside him, petting his fur. "He's scared. This dog looks asleep, but he's aware of what's happening. He doesn't know what to do because he can't move."

"Claire." Ruby's tone gentled. "We're going to have a long talk about you and your animal friends."

At the child's defense of Figg, Abbie was reminded of Jimi. With Claire on the dog's side, her concern for Figg's safety fled out the broken window.

As if someone had fired the starter's pistol, Abbie's pulse sped up. With Mr. Dubois's agreement to take Claire and Pauline to France, like ducks lining up, plans for Abbie and her mother to leave this timeline fell into place. "Mr. Dubois, that dog needs to be released in a nearby copse. If you are agreeable to this arrangement, the butler will arrange to move Lady Ashford and the dog to your basket. While that is done, you'd best work on enlarging your *montgolfière.*"

"*Oui,* I will take Lady Ashford and her maid, *Mademoiselle* Claire, and *Madam* Ruby, but not that *monstre.*" Mr. Dubois pointed to the dog. "Who is his owner?"

"Our enemy." Ruby's scathing glance rested on Abbie.

"*Quoi?!*" His voice spiked.

Abbie glowered at Ruby. "It'll only be for a short distance. If you want to take Claire, you must take the dog and release him into the woods. Once he awakens, he will return to his master."

"I do not understand your thinking, *mademoiselle.*" Mr. Dubois shook his head. "Why would you want to send such a weapon back into the hands of our enemy?"

"We have our reasons." Abbie held her breath, praying Ruby would not interfere. Ruby's silence was a welcome boon. "Those are our terms."

"Very well." Mr. Dubois released a heavy sigh before he turned to Claire. "He will be your responsibility, *mademoiselle,* while onboard my vessel."

"I will help her, Papa." Aubin tiptoed toward the dog.

Abbie rose. One duck in place, four more to go.

Ruby seemed to have learned her lesson about the danger of changing the past. She'd prevented Abbie from interfering with Robert's arrest. Her one blind spot remained with Nevin.

Abbie used Hafgufa to speak to Ruby. *"If you kill Nevin after we leave, it could alter the future Mother and I return to."*

Ruby also stood, but she crossed her arms, her chin firming as if in objection.

Abbie's mother stood between them, joining in the silent conversation. *"I'll chat with her about it."* Margaret took Ruby by the hand and led her aside. "There are a few things I want to hear about before we part."

Excellent. Two ducks in place, three to go.

Mr. Dubois hurried out of the room, no doubt to enlarge his basket, while his son stayed with Claire. The two were whispering beside the sleeping Figg. Abbie tapped Claire's shoulder, wiggling her fingers twice. Time to undo the impact she'd had on Claire's artifacts.

The girl followed her with her valise.

Once out of earshot of the others, Abbie knelt to speak to Claire. "May I see the items in your case?"

Claire opened up her valise to display her horde like a dragon showing off her gold.

"Thank you." These artifacts responded to Abbie because they recognized her as the Grimm Guardian. That was not supposed to happen for another two hundred years, when Abbie first came into her talent.

She gazed inside the bag, and the items chattered to her. She held up her hand. *"Shhh. I want all of you to go to sleep until I awaken you next. Respond when your Grimm requests your services, but you will not speak. Will you do that?"*

The items quieted inside the valise, shifting and settling down. Their easy acceptance was like a warm hug from good friends. Abbie shut the case and returned it to Claire. "Keep these safe, Claire."

"I will." She hugged the valise.

"Good girl. Now, stay close to Aubin while I check on Pauline."

Sending off the child, Abbie hurried out of the great room. Spotting the butler, she called him over. "There's been a change of plans. We will no longer need the carriage. Use it for yourselves after we've gone."

"I thought Lady Ashford needed to leave this castle soon, miss?"

"Yes, but she'll be traveling another way. First, there's an unusually large dog in the great room that needs to be taken to the hot-air balloon basket that's in the back courtyard. Then send up men to carry your mistress to the same basket. It will take her where Lord Ashford's cousin cannot find her."

"Will that be safe, miss?" His tone rose, but at her firm nod, he nodded. "As you wish."

One last duck to dispatch. She stroked it under its chin as she hurried upstairs. Time to speak to Pauline about Robert, as the seashell artifact had advised her.

*"Tell her to seek out her love."*

The moment she'd heard the words, her Grimm instincts had hummed in accord that this was something she must do. Yet, she'd dodged this talk for so long that she'd almost lost the opportunity. Pauline could have died today without Abbie ever having made her appeal.

Where would that have left Robert? She firmed her back. Abbie had been searching for a way to do this since, as a ten-year-old, she stumbled over Robert's forgotten grave and decided he was lonely.

Just because, as an adult, she'd grown to love Robert, to rely on him to guide her, and to keep her and her kids safe, didn't mean she could shirk this duty now. If she did, she'd be dishonoring all that he'd taught her.

Though it was bright outside, inching toward noon, Pauline's room was dark and quiet, with a sliver of light coming from a lone candle on the mantle. Lucy sat beside her mistress.

Bags and a small chest were packed and ready.

"How is she doing?" Abbie moved closer to the bed.

Lucy brushed away her tears. "She wakes in fits and starts, miss. My lady is in much pain."

Nodding, she sent the girl off to take the baggage downstairs and into the basket moored in the south garden. She then took a deep breath and sat on the bed.

Pauline opened pain-glazed eyes. "What is happening?"

"We're taking you to safety. Farther than London. You will travel to France to stay with Claire's family."

"I will not leave Robert!"

Abbie hardened her heart against easing Pauline's grief. "Do you want his last days to be fraught with worry?"

Pauline gulped, tears flooding her eyes.

"You can send word to him later that you are well and taking care of Claire. That will give him a modicum of peace, to know you are safe and have a purpose that will help you carry on without him."

Tears poured down Pauline's cheeks.

# Chapter Twelve

A tap sounded on the door before the butler entered Pauline's bedroom, followed by two men carrying a makeshift cot.

"We'll be just a moment." Abbie turned back to Pauline, her pulse hammering. Say it. Quickly.

"What is it?" Pauline wiped her wet cheeks.

"It's about Robert."

Pauline blinked, sniffing. "What about him?"

"His spirit has been watching over me and my children for the past three years." Tears burned Abbie's eyes. "He has done a splendid job of it, my lady, keeping us all safe. But he is lonely. He needs you and your daughter. Yet, he will not leave me. In the future, after you have left this life, will you promise to come for him in my time?"

Pauline remained silent, her tears drying as she held Abbie's gaze. "I do not know how I could even make such a promise. Even if I could, I wouldn't. My husband is a man of honor. If he feels an obligation to you, I cannot persuade him otherwise."

"Yet, you must."

Pauline took a breath and then cringed, as if that small motion had caused great discomfort. "Not if his duty to you is incomplete."

"He has taught me to be brave, my lady. To fight like a soldier to protect those I love, and to be cautious." Abbie's words faltered. At this rate, she'd convince herself she couldn't let him go.

"He did the same with me." Pauline's lips turned up in a wry smile. "Even inside this fortress." Then her face grew grave.

"Yet, we unwittingly invited a serpent to enter and strangle our child."

Abbie cleared her throat. Her mission was to safeguard the world against Nevin. This trip had taught her that. And if the only way she could give Robert peace was to end Nevin once and for all–she straightened her back–she would do it swiftly, and without mercy. "Rest assured, I will deal with that snake."

"Then I will fetch Robert when it's time." Pauline held Abbie's gaze, her lips trembling. "Give him my love?"

"Most assuredly." Abbie took Pauline's uninjured hand. The lady's grip on her fingers tightened. From their clasp, a shiver sped up Abbie's arm. The sensation was akin to a Standard Bearers' fist-bump. No celestial light spark, but she gained the impression they'd just made a sacred pact.

Pauline would come to get Robert, and Abbie was certain that the quake at their touch meant this agreement had been granted Heaven's blessing. That meant the countdown to the end of her time with Robert had begun.

She stood, her heart already aching. The ten-year-old within her hugged her tight, cutting off Abbie's breath. *Thank you!*

How was it possible for one's heart to both break and mend all at the same moment? Pinching her lips, her nose prickling, she directed the footmen to take Pauline.

"Gently!" She hovered over the procedure, and every time Pauline winced, Abbie flinched. They carried the lady out the door with great care.

Lucy returned, and while Abbie picked up the carpetbag and a portable medicine chest, the maid carted the last luggage piece downstairs.

In the castle's south courtyard, three burners fed three enormous expanded balloons. Sturdy cords tied the balloons to a basket, which was moored to the ground with pegs. The basket now spanned three times its original length and twice its width. Intricately designed handholds embellished the basket's latticework.

Abbie moved closer to Mr. Dubois. "Is this an airship?"

"What is an airship, *mademoiselle?*" He gave her a quizzical look.

"Never mind." She'd misspoken. Airships had steam engines to help direct a vessel's course, and those had yet to be invented. "How do you steer your course?"

"Like any sailing ship, my *montgolfière* is reliant on wind direction, but with a bit of magical assist to find the proper currents." His eyes twinkled as he moved his eyebrows up and down and flaunted a mischievous grin. "Or to shift the currents in the direction I require. This beautiful lady is a *montgolfière magique* in more ways than one."

A panel had fallen open to allow ingress, and the servants transported Pauline inside, while Lucy followed. They laid her cot beside a snoozing Figg, with baggage acting as a barrier between the two.

Abbie hugged Claire until the girl squirmed. She let her go with a chuckle and the child hurried into the basket after Pauline. Abbie laid a hand on the basket's railing and leaned over to check on the two. Holding Pauline's uninjured hand, the child was kneeling beside Lucy.

*"Bonjour, Mademoiselle. I am Jacques."*

Abbie's pulse thudded at the unexpected, deep male voice. This hot-air balloon had spoken to her! His invisible presence loomed like a low-lying cloud. Had she inadvertently awoken this artifact, too? Even though it didn't belong to her family?

Swallowing, she took in a shaky breath. *"Hello."*

*"Will you be traveling with us?"*

*"No, but you will take up Pauline, Ruby, Claire, and Figg, that sleeping dog."*

*"The chien is filthy. He dirties my floor."* Jacques sounded as if he had often had passengers who ignored his need for cleanliness.

*"I'm sorry about that."* Abbie's lips curved up at his lofty tone. Jacques sounded so like Nica irritated by Abbie leaving crumbs on the kitchen table. *"I am fond of Figg and want him safe. He won't be with you for long."*

*"I will watch over him. And the others. I wish to please the Grimm Guardian. Are you certain you will not travel with us? I can show you magnificent sceneries."*

*"Not today. Jacques, have you spoken to anyone else?"*

*"Non. This is an unfamiliar experience. Would you like to hear about all that I can do? It is an extensive list."*

"Abbie!" Ruby left Margaret's side to approach her.

*"I wish I could, Jacques, but I must be going. I do request that you return to sleep now, please. Can you do that?"*

*"As you wish."* The presence faded away.

She turned and Ruby embraced her. "Take care of my Peggy."

"I will. You take care of yourself, Ruby. I love you and want you to stay safe." Leaning back, she looked her straight in the eyes. "Ruby, the artifacts will no longer come if you call. That ability shouldn't be active until well into the future. You can still use them, with Claire's permission."

Ruby shrugged. "Being a Grimm will have to take a back burner for a while, anyway, as I become a guardian to both Lady Ashford and Claire." Then her expression became stern. "You have a big job ahead. Don't trust Nevin. Don't underestimate him. And don't allow your soft heart to get the better of your good judgment."

"I won't." Abbie's whole body reverberated with those words. A promise was a promise. Ending Nevin was the only way to release Robert from his self-imposed guard duty over her. "His days are numbered."

"Good girl."

"Everyone back!" Mr. Dubois waved to the gawking servants. Ruby entered the basket, and he followed, shutting the open panel. His son was still on the lawn. Aubin ran around collecting pegs.

Abbie followed her mother, a part of her squirreling away plans to visit France one day, to speak to Jacques again, in her time.

Her mother pointed toward the southeast tower entrance. "Let's watch from the battlements."

Abbie nodded. "Good idea. That will give us concealment to activate the hourglass. Arthur, end your protection over Claire."

Her ring vibrated as the link cut off. Like releasing her fierce grip on a beloved hand.

Abbie and her mother sped up the narrow stone stairs. They arrived at the top floor, out of breath. As they stepped onto the walkway, the balloons crested past them, rising ever higher.

"They're off!" Abbie waved.

"Look at Aubin clinging to that rope." Her mother hugged herself as if she were trying to hold on to him, to physically keep him from falling.

As Aubin reached for the basket, his father pulled him over the rim, and Abbie released her pent-up breath, her stomach in knots. Even though she'd seen that maneuver before, it was still hard to watch.

"Time to go, Mum." She pulled out her hourglass.

"Oh, no!" Her mother's voice was pitched low.

"What's wrong?" Abbie scanned the horizon where the hot-air balloons sailed south, afraid Aubin had fallen after all. No, he was all right.

"Look over there." Margaret pointed downward, past the castle, near the woods in the east.

Nevin, standing beside his carriage on a narrow back road, released a lightning bolt straight toward the *montgolfière*.

The strike hit the outermost balloon with a deafening *bang*, and it burst into flames.

Abbie moaned and grabbed at the stone wall ahead of her. This was her worst nightmare come to life.

"They're going to die!" Her mother's voice shook.

The flaming balloon set off the one beside it. Like a cannon blast, that one went up in flames, too.

"Only one left." Abbie's chest squeezed like a tightening vice. "I have to do something."

Inside the basket, Ruby slung her arm back as if she were about to fling something.

"She's going to kill him with a wish bomb." Abbie wanted to look away, but couldn't. "That blast could take out half the castle and the people in it."

"She won't hurt Nevin." Her mother's answer was firm. "I impressed on her how it could change the timeline and leave you and me in the future without our loved ones. She gave me her word she wouldn't kill him in this past."

And her mother had believed Ruby? In the basket, Ruby did lower her arm, with no blast sounding.

Abbie breathed out. Thank goodness, but that basket was still in trouble. "Maybe my cord can extend far enough to grab it before it falls?"

*"I can't."* Hafgufa's assertion sent Abbie's spirits plummeting. *"It's too far away."* Then the hourglass flipped over in her hand, all on its own.

Abbie clenched the hourglass. "Yousef must have activated this in our time."

Her mother tilted her head toward the time portal that had opened behind them. A *whoosh* of air dragged them toward the time tunnel.

Margaret's grip on Abbie's hand tightened. "They'll be all right, Abbie." The fear, the trembling in her tone, was missing. She sounded firm and poised.

"What are you talking about?" Abbie shook off her mother's hold, but Margaret held on tight. The last intact hot-air balloon was still afloat, but with only one to support it, the craft moved slower, and sank lower. They were a sitting target. Sweat trickled down her forehead and back as she held her breath, waiting for Nevin's next strike.

A streak of lightning shot across the air, straight at the last balloon. Abbie gulped as his strike flew past. The blast fizzled before it struck its target.

"They've moved out of his range." Abbie *whooped.*

"It's time to leave." Her mother tugged Abbie toward the portal. She tapped her chest. "I know they're safe."

Just as she spoke, a new balloon popped up above the basket, and then another. Jacques could indeed do more than shift air currents. He could repair himself. "Go, Jacques!"

"Who's that?" Margaret stepped into the portal.

Abbie followed, relief washing over her.

As soon as they were both inside, the portal opening shut off the timeline to the past.

Abbie chuckled. "Jacques is the *montgolfière*."

"Abbie, you shouldn't talk to every artifact you find."

"Whatever you say, Mum. Now we're in here, we'd better picture my sitting room." She didn't want to end up in the wrong location again.

In no time, the portal shoved Abbie and her mother out of it, feet-first. They landed inside St. Michael's cottage, in her sitting room, and the portal shut behind them.

Yousef stood beside the couch, the pink-sand hourglass clenched in his fist. "You made it! We didn't wait too long. It was almost exactly twenty-four hours when I turned over that hourglass."

"Perfect timing." Abbie raced over and hugged him tight. Yousef was real. They were home! "Thank you!"

Nica flung herself at Abbie. "You're home!"

She caught her little girl up in time for Jimi to race toward them. Kneeling, she held both her kids and breathed in their familiar scents. Strawberry on jam-mad Jimi and cleaning wipes on her clean-mad girl made her giggle. She might as well have landed in heaven instead of in Chipstead.

"Mistress Ruby is not with you, Miss Grimshaw?" Robert

limped forward. Frown lines marred his handsome forehead. Abbie released the kids, and ignoring his preference for avoiding affectionate displays, she embraced him. "I'm so glad to see you."

She inhaled his wonderful scent of beeswax and rosemary, but also received a whiff of the live Robert she'd met.

Her ghostly Robert did not pull away. His arms held her tight. As if she were both treasured and loved.

"May I inquire what's brought on this affectionate return?" His tone had a humorous lilt. He loosened his hold to lean back. "And why are you both in clothing from my time?"

Abbie memorized every part of his dear face. "We met Pauline. She sends her love."

Robert absorbed that heavy data dump in silence, his face still, eyes narrowed.

The entire Standard Bearers' crew was in Abbie's sitting room. They had gathered to call her home. Their warm welcome embraced her.

Talin skirted the coffee table to reach her. "What were you two doing in England in the 1800s?"

"Yes." Yousef set his hourglass on a side table before facing her with an inquiring glance. "I thought Ruby stole you to take you to 1700s France."

"Abbie was thinking about Robert as we left." Her mother nodded toward the earl. "That steered us to his time instead. Ruby was apoplectic."

Abbie caught Robert's gaze. His last words to her before she left in the time portal had changed their trajectory. "You mentioned your daughter just before the gate closed."

He nodded. "As the portal pulled you in, I saw Lizzy

standing beside you. But that couldn't have been, could it?" A crease formed on his forehead. "When did you arrive in England?"

"June 1816." The words came out in a whisper. It was as hard to talk to Robert about having seen him alive as it had been to be with him during his arrest.

"Lizzy was dead by then." His tone grew grave. "That's when they arrested me. We met at St. Michael's!"

"You remember?" Abbie took his hand, squeezing it. "Why did you never mention that we'd met back then?"

He shook his head. "I did not recall meeting you back then, Miss Grimshaw, though now that memory is clear."

"You must have changed the past!" Judith, who'd followed behind Talin, raised her hand at her throat. "What else might be different that we're unaware of?"

"We tried to limit any impact on our future." Abbie released Robert and stroked her kids' heads. She was back with these two. How much of the past could they have changed? "It was hard, especially after we clashed with our enemy."

"You fought him?" Robert clutched his walking stick as if to keep himself steady. "The villain was there in my time?"

She met his gaze and gulped. "Not only was he there, he struck at Pauline."

He caught Abbie in a fierce grip. "She was hurt?"

Abbie pried his grip from her forearm, but held onto his hand. "Before we left, I tended to her wounds and ensured she would be safely transported away from your castle to France."

Talin's question sprang out next. "Why there?"

"All of you have much to discuss and plan." Margaret headed for the door at a brisk pace. "I need to speak to John."

Abbie's mother was right about their need to plan, but Abbie wasn't ready for that work yet. Her legs were shaky and her mind was exhausted. But there was an issue her mother had not considered.

"Mum!" She hurried after Margaret, who was already halfway to the front door. "Until we resolve the threat from the current Earl of Ashford, you shouldn't travel around alone."

"The earl?" Yousef's tone rose as he dashed after them. "What does he have to do with any of this?"

Abbie sent him a backward glance. Nevin was his mentor. Aside from Robert, this news affected him the most.

"He is the enemy we seek." Robert's tone was clipped and vengeful as he appeared by the front door, blocking Margaret's exit. "Pauline wrote to me when I was in prison to be wary of him. To not trust Nevin if he came by to offer help."

Abbie stopped beside her mother. "We have much to discuss. Later." She hadn't even mentioned yet about Nevin confessing to killing Lizzy. That might be why the child had appeared inside the time tunnel. Her spirit could have directed Abbie to her father's time to identify her killer.

"I can drive your mother home." Yousef offered. Which would also give him time to grill Margaret about Nevin. Might be for the best. Abbie had enough on her plate with Robert.

"Unnecessary." Margaret tugged out of Abbie's hold.

"Thoroughly necessary." Abbie firmed her hold.

Judith arrived beside them in a rush, accompanied by Talin, Nica, and Jimi.

"Yousef, why don't you drive Mrs. Grimshaw in her car," Judith suggested, "and I'll follow in Shahay, if she'll let me drive her, and we can pick up groceries on the way back."

Margaret sighed. "If you both insist."

"That's a grand plan, but wait a moment." In observing her mother's distracted gaze, Abbie's instincts insisted she was missing something important. She squeezed her mother's hand. "What's wrong?"

"I can put nothing past you, can I?" With a twisted smile, her mother met Abbie's gaze. "If you must know, during this journey, I realized how much I'd enjoyed being a Grimm."

"Really?" Nica's shock rode that one word, a mirror to Abbie's reaction.

"But, Nana," Jimi's head tilted, "you always say you hate anything to do with our Grimm work."

Margaret stood straight, her head held up, the warrior Grimm she'd once been.

"Mum, do you want to take up your Grimm calling again? Join our Standard Bearers' group?"

"No. I don't know. Would you object?"

Abbie considered the question. What would it be like if, along with her Standard Bearers, a second Grimm, a fierce one, was by her side when she next faced Nevin?

A loud and vibrant, *Hooray!* rang out within her.

"Let me put it this way." A smile teased at her lips. "If you ever need to use any of our artifacts, just call and it will come to you."

"Thank you." Her mother's eyes crinkled in a smile and a blush stole up her cheeks. "I need to talk to your father first. And your brothers. I'll let you know."

Yousef winked at Abbie as he followed her mother out the front door. Judith glanced at Abbie and raised her arms in a helpless gesture before rushing after them to the car park.

# Chapter Thirteen

Abbie locked her front door and faced the others.

"What now?" Jimi stayed glued to her side. Not even the lure of his video games drew him away.

Nica, too, stayed put beside Robert and Talin.

"I need to get clean." Abbie took Nica's hand before she turned to the males. "Jimi, would you please help Talin and Robert research historical records on what happened to Pauline and Ruby since we left them and a young girl named Claire who might be with them? It won't be easy, since they might have all changed their names."

All three nodded and headed to the sitting room.

Abbie squeezed Nica's hand. "Would you be a doll and fetch me a change of clothing?"

"I cleaned your room while you were gone." Nica dashed up the stairs. "I know where everything is."

Soon, Abbie lay in the tub, hot water turning her body lethargic and her mind numb. Once she was wrinkly, and the water had cooled, she dried off, brushed her teeth, and changed before heading upstairs to her bedroom. All was quiet in the house and she slipped under her bedcovers. It was still early afternoon, but she was bone tired. A brief nap should revive her for the upcoming discussions.

Before nodding off, she sent a text to Callum to let him know she was home.

His reply was instant. *"Glad you're ok, and thanks for saving Figg."*

The pup had survived. A smile touched her heart.

*"Dinner tomorrow."* She thumbed, lying back. *"Your place. I'll cook."*

*"We'll cater, lass."*

Abbie turned over, chuckling. She cuddled into her pillow and the mobile slipped from her fingers.

The scent of a Thai dish had her mouth watering before she opened her eyes. That smelled like one of Judith's delicious meals. Had she returned already?

Abbie stretched, noting how dark her bedroom had grown. A glance out the window suggested it was well past sundown. She sat up. Why hadn't anyone woken her? Robert wasn't even by her window, standing guard.

The urge to race downstairs to join her family and friends was overwhelming, but a need to know what had happened to Claire kept her bed-bound.

Sitting cross-legged, she held open her arms. "Klaus." Her Grimm book shimmered into her hold. She snuggled the book and kissed it. "I missed you!"

The book fluttered his pages.

"Klaus, where were you in 1816?"

She received an image of the inside of Claire's valise.

"How could you have fit in there?"

The book shrank to a quarter his size.

Struck speechless, she whistled.

Klaus returned to his normal size.

"Clever." She then sent up a prayer that Claire had lived a good, long life. "Now, show me Claire's first entry."

Klaus fluttered his pages until he landed on a story describing the adventures of a young lady and her governess. They were visiting a vineyard in France, where a fairy was terrorizing farm hands by turning them into donkeys.

Abbie determined to read this fun story to her kids. Best of all, this meant both Claire and Ruby had not only survived, but thrived.

She couldn't recall ever reading this story. Like Robert's memories, Klaus had also changed, adding new tales.

"What about Pauline? Have you any tales about her?"

The book lay still on her lap. Abbie shuddered at that lack of response. Hopefully, Talin had more luck with his research into Pauline. Before her next question, she held herself steady, her core crunched. "Where is Nevin?"

The book didn't move. Now this she understood. Nevin would have set up protection spells to hide himself, which likely blinded Klaus. Shrugging off those two setbacks, she opened to a blank page. Then, taking a deep breath, she regurgitated the dark energy Hafgufa shunted into her when she broke Nevin's *Keep-out* spell over Claire's burning home.

Klaus used that power to record the tale of Abbie's recent adventures. When she'd expunged it all, her stomach unknotted. She was finally truly clean. Abbie set the book aside–Klaus was still busy writing–and grabbed her mobile.

She needed to set the wheels in motion to gain more ammunition on Nevin and knew just the source to tap. Kiros.

"Abbie!" Kiros answered on the first ring, his voice sounding chipper. "This is a lovely surprise. What may I do for you?" His light tone picked up a smile. "Do you have another submerged ship you wish recovered?"

His good mood left her dispirited. This immortal had lied to her. Repeatedly. After she'd offered him her hand in friendship. "Evening, Kiros. I'd like us to meet tomorrow."

He went silent, perhaps picking up on her cross tone. When he spoke, his humor had fled the scene. "What about?"

"Your son. Text me where and when."

She hung up and headed downstairs. The kitchen was packed. With all seven SB crew present, they filled the space, making it both cozy and noisy. Like a Grimshaw family gathering. Their cheer was contagious. If she'd been a cat, she'd have padded and purred.

The aromas from the dishes spread out on the table spun her appetite into a frenzy. After everyone served themselves, Abbie turned to Talin. "I couldn't find any stories about Pauline in Klaus. You?"

Talin moved his tablet aside to make room for his plate. "Nothing about Pauline Blackburn or Mrs. Livingston."

Abbie glanced at Robert, who leaned against the back door, head down, ankles crossed.

"She hid herself right proper." Jimi dug into his meal.

"Nothing other than her death notice in London, same as before you left." Talin topped up his wineglass.

Abbie's chest tightened. Pauline couldn't have died. Her appetite fled, and Abbie moved her fork through her food.

"Until a year later."

She snapped her head up and spotted Talin's grin.

Robert's eyes sparkled. "I had Mr. Higgins search under Paul Black. That was her *nom de plume*. He uncovered a sculpture displayed in a remote French museum, a year after Pauline's supposed death. Of three fairies protecting a young girl. Seems Black became quite prolific, producing several pieces a year over the next fifty years. Those pieces have been sold worldwide, and each is considered a collector's item."

"They're terrible teases." Judith rolled her eyes. "I told them you'd been through enough."

Abbie didn't care. Waves of joy encompassed her. She hadn't messed up the timeline. This was the best news.

"Your turn, Miss Grimshaw," Robert bowed to her, "to share your adventure."

With a nod, she began her telling.

By the time she finished answering questions, all of their plates were empty. The only story she left out was her last talk with Pauline.

They set into their dessert, and the room grew quiet.

Abbie stood and collected the empty dishes. "Shall we move to the comfort of the sitting room?"

"It's late." Judith tipped her head toward the children.

"I don't want to go to bed yet!" Nica's lips pressed in a pout, her hands gripping the table's edge. "This is just getting good. You're going to talk about what we should do about Robert's cousin next."

Jimi's face took on a matching, stony expression. "If you make us go, we'll eavesdrop." He crossed his arms. "The fireplace is good at sharing EVERYTHING it hears. So, you might as well let us stay downstairs."

It was well past their bedtime, but this discussion was too important. "Alright."

"Yay!" Jimi pumped his fists in the air.

After the dishwasher was running, they re-convened in the sitting room. Abbie sat on the sofa bracketed by her kids, her favorite position. Robert stood by the window, his thoughtful gaze fixed on the quiet night. Yousef, Talin, and Judith lounged on chairs, drinking wine or sipping tea.

"First, we need to know what Robert remembers of the demon expulsion from Spain." Abbie caught and held his gaze.

"And why have you never mentioned that before?" Yousef's question was a mirror of the one elbowing her.

Robert strolled over and sat on the sofa armrest closest to Nica. "It's as if Miss Grimshaw mentioning it at supper unlocked a memory. Now those events are as clear as if they had happened this morning."

He shimmered, fading in and out. Since Robert didn't blink or react, he likely didn't even realize he'd done that. His gaze wandered as if he were lost in that long-ago event. "Even though the door to the underworld was only open a sliver, demons had escaped through it. And someone appeared to be working to widen the gap."

"Who?" Yousef leaned forward, elbows on his knees, his glass of wine cupped in his hands. "Your cousin?"

"The priest did not say." Robert shimmered again.

Talin stood and came up behind Robert to run his hand across his back until the ghost's essence steadied and became clearer. It was as if Talin had fed Robert energy to help him stay stable and whole.

Abbie gave a grateful nod to Talin.

He winked back and returned to his seat, while Robert sat up, as if he'd received a bolt of strength. "Once we began the ceremony, demons set upon us."

Abbie shivered at the vision Robert wove. Demons were deceitful and dangerous. "How did you fight them off?"

"The priest had blessed our weapons. We not only fought off those devils, but killed every one of them."

Robert rubbed his injured leg, but he no longer

shimmered. "One impaled me before I killed it. Once we dispatched the last of them, we finished the ritual."

"What did that ritual involve, exactly?" Judith asked.

"Each man had to sacrifice an item they held most dear. I offered my mother's pendant. We then spoke words of power that are imprinted in my memory. After the gate shut, the priest swore us to silence. So, no one else would be tempted to open another such foul gate."

Judith passed him her notebook and pen. "If Nevin opens another gate, we'll need those words."

Robert set to writing.

"This was the battle where you were injured." Abbie tiptoed across this sensitive subject. "Talin's research suggested an enemy battalion had attacked and that you'd lost a few men in the skirmish."

Robert handed the pad and pen back to Judith. "Those reports had it wrong. In their defense, army commanders are known to falsify records to hide inexplicable or unsavory news. Also, while it's true only a few died during our encounter with the demons, days later, an assassin ambushed my company. The villains murdered every one of my men while they slept. Even the priest, who was due to depart the next day. I, too, would have perished, except I'd been sent to a hospital in England by then."

Judith tore off the written page before she put away her pad and pen. "This spell has a silencer built into it. Which explains why you failed to share your demon experience with us earlier. The priest not only made you swear to stay quiet, but backed it with a magical compulsion to do so."

"Why am I able to speak of it now, then?" Robert shook

his head, as if he had difficulty accepting her theory.

"The why is immaterial." Yousef's jaw worked, as if he ground his teeth. "What matters is who opened that gate, and who ambushed your troop?"

Judith passed the spell sheet to Yousef.

With barely a glance at the page, he handed it off to Jimi, who was closest to him. Not surprising, since Yousef cared little for magic.

The boy sat back, yawning, and read the spell. He then held up the spell sheet, fluttering it. "When this spell closed that underworld gate, the mage who opened it was cross. He tried to stop the spell working, but couldn't."

Everyone gaped at Jimi in silence.

"Thank you, Jimi." Abbie took the sheet he offered her. "After committing that atrocity in Spain, I believe the Roman came to England to seek revenge against Robert, the last surviving member of that company. He assumed your cousin Nevin's identity, killed your daughter, and framed you for the killing. After your death, he stole your title. Which is why he is now the current Earl of Ashford."

Yousef groaned and slumped back in his chair.

Robert's breath hissed out. "One thing puzzles me. Kiros said Pyramus was our enemy. Does this mean Nevin is an immortal? Is he Pyramus?"

Abbie took up that question. "No, but he is related to Kiros. The mage that Ruby wounded in 1703 wore a medallion. It had Kiros's face on it, suggesting Nevin is his son."

"Cripes!" Talin cried out.

Abbie understood his consternation. He wouldn't want his friend Kiros involved with Nevin's villainy.

Also, Yousef had once told Abbie he wanted to be like the earl, as generous to his fellow man as the Earl of Ashford had been to him. Abbie grimaced at the shattering of his hero.

"Nevin must be stopped." Her gaze settled on Yousef and then on Talin. Where did they both stand on this course?

"He certainly isn't the man I grew up revering." Yousef's thumb drummed on his armrest. Then he met her gaze and gave a decisive nod. "I'm in."

"Me, too." Talin sighed, and it sounded as if his words came from deep within him.

However reluctantly they gave their affirmations for their next course of action, Abbie was glad to get it.

"Wow." Judith sat, wide-eyed, a hand on her chest. "This means that in stopping Nevin, we're going against the immortals, too."

Nica's normally gentle gaze turned flint hard as she shifted to face Abbie. "If Nevin killed all those soldiers and Robert's Lizzie, he's evil. But how do we stop him from hurting anyone else, Abbie? Should I summon Kali?"

Instead of using her talent to call on the goddess, Nica was learning to rely on Abbie's guidance. Her little girl was growing up. "Not yet. But we may have to, at the right time." She turned to Jimi. "Did the spell say anything else?"

The boy, who seemed half asleep, didn't bother sitting up. "It didn't like the mage interfering with it in Spain. Then, in St. Michael's, God broke its silence code. It didn't like that either. Says it won't stand for more interference." The boy snuggled against Abbie's side, feet tucked in.

Judith pointed to Robert. "Abbie said you had been praying when she came across you in the church. And an angel had spoken to you. Suggest God might have a hand in matters at the church."

Robert nodded. "Agreed."

Abbie trod carefully on her next topic, too. The kids' late mother. "Hargeet Gill spoke her prayer inside St. Michael's. And that prayer was answered by bringing us together to form the Standard Bearers. Nevin also had dealings with Hargeet. I wonder what their connection might have been about."

Judith huffed. "He could have asked her to contact a god to help him regain full power. If she failed to do that, it would explain why he ordered her killed. He probably hoped her death would cause her talent to pass to her brother. Someone easier to manipulate."

"How do demons come into this?" Talin reached for his cooling teacup. Once he touched it, tendrils of steam wafted up from the liquid. "Why does Nevin want to open a gate to the underworld to let demons into our world? How does that benefit him?"

"Demons cast dark spells." Nica took the spell sheet from Abbie. "Maybe he wants one to boost his magic."

"Interesting thought, Nica!" Abbie squeezed her hand. She was taking this talk about her late mother well. "That would explain Nevin's interest in demons."

To see what their electromagnetic wizard might make of the spell, Abbie asked Nica to pass on that sheet to Talin.

Taking up the page, he set his cup down and ran his fingers over the lettering. The sheet sparked, setting off a mini-lightning storm between his hand and the paper.

Abbie held herself rigid, half afraid that the sheet was about to burst into flames. It didn't. Talin passed it to Judith, who touched the sheet and then cried out, releasing it.

"Sorry." Talin's grin was not in the least repentant as he retrieved his teacup. "That's a feisty little spell."

Judith picked up the fallen sheet, which no longer sparked. Folding it, she tucked it into her jacket pocket. "I'll run it by Granny Chan and see if she can shed more light on its makeup."

"We've gained some important intel on our enemy." Abbie adjusted her arm against which Jimi was cuddling. "Since his injury in 1703, his powers have waned, and he's aging. He wasn't strong enough to counter the gate closure spell. And once he disguised himself as Nevin, I believe he didn't have the power to cast another disguise spell. That's why he still looks like Nevin."

"But what are we going to do with all this newfound knowledge?" Robert spread his arms, as if at a loss.

"I've contacted Kiros." Abbie stretched her legs, wiggling her toes. Her limbs had cramped from sitting still for so long. Might be time to wrap up this discussion. "I'm hoping Kiros can give me a report about Nevin's motivations and maybe some understanding about his son's interest in demons."

"Is Kiros likely to admit anything useful?" Yousef's tone was highly skeptical.

"I want to attend this meeting." Talin set his cup down with a clatter. "I could persuade him to talk."

Abbie held his earnest glance. She'd planned to use her cord to get the truth out of Kiros, but Talin's brand of persuasion, that of a caring friend, might be less intrusive than Hafgufa's coercive force. But could Talin remain objective?

Considering his impulsive, emotional, and light-hearted

character, Abbie suspected not so much. Yet, he was a Standard Bearer, and he was one of her best friends. At the meeting with an untrustworthy immortal, she wanted a powerful ally whom she wholeheartedly trusted to keep her balanced and clear-eyed.

Just as Abbie was about to answer, Ruby's parting words taunted her. *"Don't let your soft heart get the better of your good judgment."* Like a ghostly finger poking at her ribs.

Abbie shook off that uneasy touch. "I would love your company." She then turned to the others. "I also want to visit Spain, in case Nevin considers re-opening that gate."

"Brilliant." Judith quiet-clapped, her gaze resting on Jimi's sleeping form. "It wouldn't hurt to find out if Nevin has visited there recently."

Exhaustion nipped at Abbie's heels, too. Despite having taken a long nap earlier, she was ready to hit the sheets again. "Let's wrap up. We can reconvene after our conversation with Kiros." She nodded to Talin. "I'll text you as soon as I hear details of the meeting."

As her friends headed to the front door, Abbie met Robert's gaze, tilting her head toward Jimi. He came over and lifted the sleeping boy, while Abbie rose and took Nica's hand.

After settling the children in their beds, they both headed downstairs. Abbie to use the loo to wash up, and Robert to check the windows and doors were secured on the ground floor.

"Thank you for caring for Pauline." Those were his first words to her about his wife. They sounded heartfelt.

She flashed him a side glance. "I loved meeting her. She was gutsy, a fighter. I had a hard time convincing her to leave

England without you."

His answering grin was wide. "She is a lady with an independent spirit as long as the Thames. Pauline couldn't have resisted helping a child in danger, though. Not after losing Lizzy. It gives me solace to know she lived a long and productive life, with lots of people to love."

# Chapter Fourteen

A cool breeze awoke Abbie from a fitful sleep. Robert must have arrived to keep watch by her window.

She didn't bother to open her heavy-lidded eyes. "I plan to visit Callum tomorrow."

He strode closer, his limping gait alerting her to his approach in the darkened room. He sat on the edge of her bed, the mattress depressing beside her right foot, like a puppy curling down for a nap. "You have chosen him."

Not a question, but a statement, with a smile riding it. He knew her well.

She chuckled and opened her eyes to meet his crinkled gaze. "My heart chose him years ago, right after he came to our rescue at the Gill flat. A knight in shining armor galloping to rescue a damsel in distress."

Robert's grin grew wider, his teeth flashing white in the night. "You hardly needed rescuing, Miss Grimshaw. As I recall, you found and used your ring to shield yourself and the children before disaster struck."

"What mattered was that he *wanted* to rescue me."

"That happened years ago. What sealed the deal now?"

"Ruby, and my mother." Abbie stretched her arms before snuggling back under her blankets. "Ruby helped me see how I had allowed my fears to color my actions, despite advising my kids to do exactly the opposite. My mother said something similar before we left on this journey."

But Ruby had a way of getting under a girl's skin, like an annoying thorn. Too tiny to pull out, but too painful to ignore.

Abbie poked Robert's hip with her foot. "She asked me why I had never made a play for you."

"What was your response?" He now sounded sober.

"That you were a man with your eyes and heart fixed firmly on your prize."

Her response earned her a deep, sexy chuckle.

"You know me too well, Miss Grimshaw."

"I do." She settled back, sleep pulling at her when she came wide awake. "Robert, do you think Callum and I will suit each other? As well as you and Pauline?"

He grew silent, as if he were considering her question.

Not an easy, *Yes*? His silence concerned her as much as her mother's had after Abbie mentioned she might have that besotted look more than Callum. But she was no longer afraid to reach for her favorite ice cream. Hadn't she made that clear?

The longer the silence grew, the more agitated her butterflies became.

"You two are much alike." Robert's tone, when he finally spoke, was thoughtful. "Principled. Determined. Honorable. You both also have a similar goal. You want to help those in danger. But you may not always approach a situation in the same manner."

"What do you mean?"

"As Grimm Guardian, you view problems posed in that light. Your well-tuned instincts guide you toward the best solution. But not everyone views every situation the same way, Miss Grimshaw."

Abbie lay awake long after his weight vanished from beside her feet. Had Robert been speaking about her and Callum, or her and himself?

She and Robert sometimes disagreed about how to respond to trouble. They'd not agreed to her moving into this cottage with her kids, so close to where the kid's mother had been killed. Yet, she'd known that she must, to capture the demon responsible.

It was a while before she fell into a troubled sleep.

* * *

The next morning, once the kids were off to school, Abbie drove Rosie out of St. Michael's car park. Life as usual.

After a full day's shift as an EMT, she returned home in need of a refreshing bath before her date. And time to center herself.

Robert had guessed last night that she'd finally committed to Callum as her man. Deciding you loved someone and saying it aloud to that person were two vastly different things. The first made her soul hum with contentment. The second had butterflies swirling within her, as if they were caught up in a tornado.

Her parents had picked her kids up at school and taken them home, leaving Abbie free for the night. Lazing in the steaming tub of scented, bubbly water, she dialed her mother.

Margaret Grimshaw answered, and her father's voice boomed in the background. "Don't look at your brother!"

Nica giggled.

Exactly the familial sounds Abbie needed to hear. The last of her day's tension floated away.

"John's playing chess with Nica." There was a long-suffering note in her mother's tone. "He refuses to play with Jimi since he's convinced the chess pieces advise the boy on the best moves to make. Robert's helping Jimi with his homework."

A song played near her mother.

"What's that tune, Mum?"

"'*Where and When*,' by Peggy Lee." Her mother's voice grew softer, and she hummed along with the music. "It's lovely, isn't it?"

"Lovely. Thinking of Ruby, Mum? According to Klaus, she became Claire's governess and married Mr. Dubois. She ended up working for the French Grimms alongside her husband and Claire, quelling supe trouble."

"Did Ruby ever return to England?" Her mother's first question about Ruby.

"Once Claire came of age, they all moved back to England under assumed names, even Pauline. Pauline was laid to rest at St. Michael's beside her daughter and Robert." She paused a moment. "I couldn't find where Ruby was buried."

Her mother went silent again.

"If you want more specifics, Mum, Klaus can help."

Just when Abbie thought her mother wouldn't say another word, she spoke. "I'm glad I had the chance to meet her. I wouldn't have missed that opportunity for the world."

"Good to hear." The love in her mother's tone released Abbie's concerns. She relaxed into her now tepid bath, turning the hot water back on with her toes. "Kids aren't too much?"

"All is good, sweetheart. Enjoy your date."

"Talk soon, Mum."

After her bath, Abbie changed into her best "date" outfit, a black satin wrap dress with a plunging neckline, and long pirate-style sleeves worn with matching slim black satin heels.

These shoes would be terrible for chasing down a demon, but were stable enough to get her from her car to Callum's front door.

She hadn't dressed this provocatively since before she left London, before the bombing, and before taking up her life as a Grimm. But then, tonight was a momentous night. The first time she'd be confessing her romantic love to anyone.

On her arrival at Callum's place, Figg barked from inside the house.

Her ring buzzed her and her shield sprang up.

"Stand down." Abbie waited for Arthur to lower her shield before pressing the doorbell.

Her cord swirled within her right forearm, twitching at her forefinger, ready to strike out. "That goes for you, too."

*"Killjoy."* Hafgufa's sulky voice faded away.

Abbie was chuckling when Callum opened his front door. He had a firm hand on Figg's collar, holding the excited dog down, much as Abbie had restrained her two artifacts.

One look and Callum swallowed, his pupils widening.

"Were you expecting me in fatigues?" She added a teasing note to her tone. In his black suit and a gray silk shirt that exactly captured the color of his stormy gaze, he left her breathless, too.

"Your outfit is an improvement on anything I could have hoped for, lass." He made a welcoming hand gesture into his home.

Stepping inside, she handed over a bottle of Britain's best Pinot Noir Rosé and inhaled the wonderful scents drifting from the kitchen.

Callum read the label. "My favorite Kent brand."

She'd made the correct choice. Being BFFs with Callum's nephew had its perks.

After a chaste peck on her cheek, he drew away. She pulled him back for a too-long delayed, whole-hearted, no-hold-back kiss. One that she hoped would show him her feelings. They drew apart, gasping. The moment Callum was out of her hold, she missed him. She doubted she'd taste a thing tonight that would be more wonderful than his kiss.

His eyes lit up with mischief as he brushed her cheek with the back of his fingers. "I like how this evening's starting out. I take it your trip into the past was a success?" He shut and locked the door behind her.

"It helped me make a few personal decisions. Ones I hadn't realized I'd been avoiding."

"What gave you this enlightenment? Meeting Robert in the flesh?"

She raised a questioning eyebrow. Robert hadn't even crossed her mind tonight. Was Callum jealous?

He shrugged. "Talin mentioned you met him in 1816." His gaze stayed on her. "What was it like? Was he enigmatic?"

"Despite being strangers, it was like meeting an old friend."

"Hmm. We should eat first or the food will get cold." He held out his hand. "Come on into the kitchen."

"One second." She knelt to address Figg. He'd been waiting patiently, though his tail thumped violently–the only outward sign that he was as thrilled to see Abbie as she was to see him. Best of all, he didn't pull away when she hugged him. "Hello, darling."

Callum had taught Figg that an embrace wasn't something to fear. She cherished holding him close. "I'm so glad you made it home safely, Figg."

When he finally squirmed within her hold, Abbie released him and stood. "Appears, there are limits to how much affection one can stomach."

"Not in my book." Callum ruffled Figg's neck. "We've both been looking forward to your visit. His earlier barking fit was from his excitement at your arrival. Normally, he rarely barks." He took her hand.

Savoring his hold, Abbie allowed Callum to lead her into his eat-in kitchen. His fingers brushed her upper arm as he tucked her chair in and set off a shiver of awareness.

Unfortunately, Callum sat at the other end of the table. The length between them might as well have been miles instead of a few feet. Where his attention during dinner lacked in touches and kisses, he made up by seducing her taste buds.

They had cured meats and cheeses for appetizers, followed by Cullen Skink, a smoked haddock, potato, and onion soup as the main meal. Dessert was a Cranachan, made of cream and fresh raspberry layers, sprinkled with Scottish oats, and flavored with whisky.

Since he'd asked earlier, during their meal Abbie filled him in on her meeting with 1816's Robert, then her visit to Pauline, and Nevin's arrival at Ashford castle.

"And this man is the current Earl of Ashford?" Callum's hands curled into fists beside his dessert glass.

"The earl's magic and life are waning." Her gaze traveled to Figg. After gobbling down his dinner, the dog had positioned himself on the rug within easy reach of his master, no doubt hoping to score a few leftovers.

Callum petted Figg, who leaned into his touch. "How long

might he live? As long as the earl does?"

A disturbing thought. "I don't believe the two longevity spells are linked."

He leaned forward, his interest completely captured. "What makes you say that?"

"Ruby and the Grimm she worked with hurt Nevin in 1703. So much so that by the time we met him in 1816, we suspected he may have lost the power to cast another disguise spell. That's why he's stuck looking like Nevin. Whereas, Figg doesn't seem in the least affected."

The dog whimpered in inquiry and glanced at her at the mention of his name.

"He was as strong and fearsome as ever in Robert's time. As he is now. He will outlive us all." She met Callum's contemplative gaze. "I'll note in Klaus that whichever Grimm takes over after me, until eternity, must watch over Figg."

"Thank you." His whisper was steeped in gratitude, and she suspected came straight from his heart.

Meeting his gaze, she shivered. Was that the look her mother had spoken about?

"What do you intend, Abbie?" Callum glanced away, fiddling with the napkin. "To kill the earl?"

She silently absorbed the cooling of his tone, knowing she trod on dangerous ground here. Callum was a man of law and order to his core.

Whereas she was the Grimm guardian. Lives depended on how she dealt with Nevin. Demons were not meant to roam the Earth, free to slaughter unprotected humans. "Ruby told me to show the fiend no mercy. It's what I promised Pauline I would do. What I must do to protect my kids. Everyone, really."

"What does this have to do with Robert's wife?"

"I extracted her promise to come for Robert." She raised her gaze, a thrill spiraling through her at having secured that pledge from the lady.

Deep lines etched Callum's forehead, and his lips were pressed tight as he tapped the tabletop. "Does Robert know?"

She shook her head. Unease rippled over her tranquility. "Pauline insisted he wouldn't leave me until his duty was completed." She shrugged, shifting tense muscles. "That won't happen until the earl is no longer a threat."

She pushed her empty dessert glass away, her spoon rattling within it as she met his gaze, her shoulders set with determination. "We can't allow Nevin to draw demons into our world, Callum."

Resignation washed over his face, and his arms dropped to his sides. "If the police become involved in this mess, there's little chance the supe community will stay hidden."

"The authorities won't need to." Abbie's passion to share part of her plans surged. "I hope to use my podcast to rally supes to help me."

"Will they step up?" His tone was skeptical.

Understandable. There was little trust between the supe community and Grimms, but Abbie had made a few inroads into that divide. "Time will tell. We now have one stalwart friend within the supe community. The Lady of the Lake. Vivian Irvine. Maybe even a few others."

His gaze softened—as if in support of that monumental accomplishment. "I'd like to help, too. Anything I can do?"

"My first order of business is to speak to Kiros about his

son." Her appetite replete, Abbie dropped her napkin on the table. "Talin plans to accompany me. What we learn from that discussion will color how we approach Nevin."

Callum stood to collect dishes, waving her down when she rose to help. "I'm glad he'll be there to back you up."

Abbie slumped back into her seat, relishing being catered to. Callum was a gentleman. One of the many things she loved about him. "Talin and Judith are researching what the Earl's been up to since 1816. Yousef plans a frontal assault by visiting his benefactor at his castle in Ashford."

"Solid plans." That sounded like approval. Callum added her dessert glass to his collection.

"I'm also planning a visit to Spain."

He swung back, the tableware he carried rattling and clinking. His piercing glance pinned her in place. "You're going to check out the last underworld gate."

"Yes." Gentlemanly, protective, and astute. He was a man of many talents.

"Alone?"

"No. With Robert and the kids."

"You're taking–" Callum cut off whatever he was about to say and stared in silence, eyes shooting bullets. He then stomped off to the kitchen and dumped the dishes on the counter, setting off a royal clang.

Figg whined and sat up.

Abbie swallowed past a tight throat, her thoughts awhirl. What had she said wrong? Then she remembered his possible jealousy of Robert. Was he upset about...

"Is it wise to take the kids?"

Ah, not jealousy, but concern for the children's safety.

Except her kids had powers. As did Robert. And, as a working Grimm, danger came with the territory.

"With Nevin on the loose," she twirled her wineglass, "the children are safer when they're with me."

"Point taken."

Her gaze swung up. Was it? Did he truly understand?

Callum returned and sat beside her this time, taking her hand. "What if the earl follows you to Spain?"

"I was concerned about that too, when we first arrived back." She squeezed his fingers, relishing his touch. She'd missed it all night. "Then I remembered that my mother and I had an invisibility spell over us when we faced Nevin in Robert's castle. The earl shouldn't be any more suspicious of either of us now than before we left."

She held Callum's gaze, and those butterflies returned to toy with her. Love was so intoxicating.

"Sure there's nothing I can do?" he asked again.

How to answer that honestly? Her current goal was to kill Nevin. That would go against everything Callum believed in as a police officer.

A brush against her legs drew her glance to Figg. He'd moved closer to lean his face on her lap. The pup gazed up, as if he were posing the same offer. *I want to help, too.*

She stroked the dog's forehead. Now Figg would have no compunction to assisting her with her current mission. But she needed him to keep his master safe.

Taking a deep breath, she turned back to Callum. "This will be a magical fight." She tilted her head toward the dog. "Your strongest weapon and defense is Figg. Best if you two keep a low profile and watch out for each other."

Disappointment dropped in his eyes and he lowered his lashes, hiding from her. Abbie cringed at having hurt him and fished in her purse for her ace to win back his adorable smile. "Thank you for giving this to me."

Callum's eyes lit up at the sight of the compass artifact in her palm. "Levi!"

Figg licked the metal.

"*Ew!*" Levi's tone was loaded with disgust.

Abbie chuckled and wiped the compass on her napkin. "He came in very handy." She tucked it into Callum's hand. "In case of trouble, use Levi to find your way to me."

His gaze held hers, and then he leaned in for a kiss. It was the softest of touches, yet one that both claimed her and set her soaring.

He released her far too soon.

Abbie cleared her throat, the words *I love you* blocking her airway.

He released her and stood. "Head into the sitting room. I'll put on the kettle."

Her cheeks infused with heat, Abbie did as he bid. Figg followed her as she prowled the front room, checking out the windows. All was quiet inside and out. Finally, she sank onto a loveseat and kicked off her heels.

Figg, who'd followed her on her prowl, lay across her feet. Sighing in pleasure at his warm presence, her gaze skimmed the room again until it landed on the piano. Callum's fingers had once tickled those ivories when she'd been searching for a particular tune. For a norm, he could be surprisingly helpful with her Grimm cases.

Callum returned with the tea tray. "Want me to play?"

"I'd love it!" She spoke with sincerity.

Sipping her tea, her butterflies having settled down, Abbie enjoyed his rendition of Shahay's mournful tune. While the fae car's version thrummed with healing power, Callum's wasn't as magical, but it was evocative. Like the man. When he reached the last notes, Figg set to barking.

Abbie's pulse shot up with the dog's alarm.

Figg raced for the front door and she went after him. "Arthur, shields up over Callum and me. Use his tie pin as your touch point."

Callum was at her heels. "Figg wouldn't bark unless there's a threat."

They stopped by the door. "Arthur's protecting you, but stay behind me."

He hesitated, and then nodded. "Will do. Figg, sit, stay quiet, and out of sight."

The dog whined in protest, but did as his master ordered. Except, he sat in front of Callum, as if determined to protect him with his body if he couldn't do it with his barks.

Abbie squared her shoulders before opening the door.

A man in a chauffeur's uniform stood on the doorstep.

Behind him, a platinum gray Peugeot was parked on the drive, eclipsing Rosie. The house security lights lit up the night, but the vehicle's tinted windows hid who had arrived.

That blinding didn't deter Abbie. She recognized the vehicle. Nevin had come to call.

A shudder of dread flew down her spine.

The chauffeur offered her a manila envelope.

Callum reached past her and took the offering, ripping it open. He gave it a scan and then shoved it back at the driver.

"That's not happening."

"He's right there." The man pointed to a snarling Figg. "You can't deny you've stolen him from his lordship."

"I found this dog." Abbie used a commanding tone. "I couldn't locate the owner, and since DCI Radford was looking for a pet, I gave him the dog. He wasn't stolen."

"How you gained the dog is immaterial." Clutching his manila envelope in a fist, the man's scathing glance and tone were implacable. "Figg belongs to the earl, and he wants him back. Now." He leaned forward to grab the dog.

Figg lunged at him, teeth bared.

The fellow barely retreated in time to keep his fingers.

Callum drew papers from a nearby cupboard drawer and waved them. "I've registered my dog with the local Kennel Club. He's microchipped. I also have veterinary records that prove he's mine. What proof do you have?"

Of course, Callum had planned for this contingency. Time she made some preparations.

# Chapter Fifteen

Holding her hand behind her back, Abbie called in Kenny, her magic-identifying spectacles. The specs filled her palm, and she put them on to get a better lay of the land.

The specs shaded the scenery in pink and confirmed the chauffeur was a norm. Not a threat. As for the earl's car, it was covered in shades of darkness, suggesting a stronger shield than tinted windows.

*"Hafgufa. Can you break that barrier?"*

*"It will take time."*

*"Start now, while we delay."* She sent the cord out of her finger and toward the car in a thin line of gold.

Could Kenny escort the earl and his Peugeot, shield and all, straight to the underworld? A tempting thought. That would end this fight. Right now.

*"Kenny, can we do that?"*

*"No, Abbie."* His reply was flat. *"Not past that shield."*

The chauffeur waved toward the vehicle. "That dog will answer to his lordship's call."

*"FIGG, COME HERE!"*

At that familiar voice in her head, terror thrummed along Abbie's nerves.

Figg stayed put, but he shivered.

"You're upsetting my dog." Callum reached past Abbie and shoved the door closed.

The driver blocked it with his booted foot.

"I'm sorry his lordship lost his pet." Callum's pressure on the door didn't waver. The intensity on his face was frightening.

He was petrified of losing Figg.

A whine from Figg drew Abbie's glance to the pup.

Figg stared at Callum with the same terror in his gaze. He was frightened for Callum's safety. That he might lose him, as he'd lost the boy he once loved, before Nevin slew him.

"My pup doesn't belong to his lordship." With each word Callum uttered, the driver's face grew redder. "Contact the RSPCA. Though by now, his dog might have been euthanized."

The driver speared Figg with a furious glance before he drew back his foot. The door slammed shut in his face. He stomped away, his footsteps echoing ominously.

Abbie texted Talin, Judith, and Yousef with her thumbs. *S.O.S. Callum's house.*

Callum paced behind her. "What are we going to do?"

"Hafgufa is working to break the shield over the car."

He ran his hand through his hair. "How will that help?" His lips were trembling, and Figg was quaking. All that mattered to these two was each other's safety.

"If I can get past his shield, my specs could send him straight to the underworld."

"Can you do that?" Callum came to a halt beside her. Then he gulped. "Will he be able to survive there?"

The question threw Abbie. Amid his crisis, he worried about Nevin's well-being? That thought hadn't even crossed her mind. But his question reminded her of Robert's words. Not everyone saw the same situation in the same way. While she was focused on saving all of humanity, Callum still saw the world in shades of law and order. Right and wrong.

"Anything's possible." While she didn't know how to

handle her and Callum's differing worldviews, she could save his dog.

She knelt and called the pup to her. "Figg, Callum's shielded. He's safe. Now hold still while I protect you. Arthur, use his collar as your touchpoint to shield Figg."

"Good!" Callum patted her back. "That's good. He can't take Figg if he has your shield over him."

The ring's energy flared, sweeping over Figg.

"COME NOW!" Nevin's shout reverberated inside Abbie's head. This time, an image of Callum blasted by one of Nevin's lightning bolts accompanied the order.

Abbie tightened her hold on Figg's neck fur. "Don't listen to him. He can't hurt Callum."

Figg whined and then vanished despite her grip on his neck fur.

"No!" Callum's shout was drenched with devastation and his hand encountered empty air where Figg had been.

"Arthur!"

*"My shield is still around him."*

Abbie sprang to her feet, pulled the front door open, and rushed outside in time to see Figg jump inside the earl's car through its open back door. The door shut and Arthur's protection over the dog cut off.

The vehicle's wheels squealed as it sped away.

Abbie ran after the car barefoot, her cord still attached to the vehicle. "Hafgufa, stop that car!"

The Peugeot's brakes screamed as the car struggled to race off while her cord worked to pull it back. Then the car seemed to jerk, then it swerved onto the main road.

*"He sliced off my hold on the car!"* Hafgufa sounded livid.

Abbie's steps slowed.

Callum rushed past her, sprinting down the road.

The car vanished into the night.

Out of breath, and defeated, Abbie stopped, retracting Hafgufa. She mentally reviewed her artifacts for one she could use. A wish bomb could take Nevin out, but it would also take out Figg, and nearby homes, and the people within them. Basil could help her fly, but what good would that do?

She knew where Nevin was likely headed. Home to Ashford. He'd had a couple of hundred years to booby trap that place and set up barriers to intruders. And without Figg's cooperation, how was she to save the dog?

Callum finally stopped far down the road, and then he screamed into the night.

Down the lane, windows opened and people looked out, calling out in concern.

He trudged back, waving off offers of help from his neighbors. "Why? Why would Figg leave me for him?"

Abbie took his hand. It was icy cold. "The earl threatened to roast you. Figg left to protect you. He didn't believe my shield was strong enough to keep you safe."

Impotent to help Callum, she led him back toward his home. "Come on. I have an idea how to track Figg."

Once they were back in the sitting room and on the loveseat, she held out her arms. "Klaus, come."

The book settled over her open arms.

"Show me Figg."

Callum sucked in his breath, leaning over her shoulder to look at the book.

Klaus flipped open his cover and pages turned before he

showed her the inside of an empty dog house.

"That's Figghouse." Abbie pointed to the drawing. "It's how Figg refers to it. It's where he stayed when he lived with Nevin. I've visited that castle, albeit in the past. Figghouse seems to be on the south lawn." Where the hot-air balloon had moored.

Callum flicked the diagram with the back of his hand. "Figg's not there now."

"Nevin's shielded his car so Klaus couldn't get past it to see inside the vehicle, but the book is showing us where Nevin plans to take Figg."

Callum jumped to his feet. "Then that's where we should go."

"No." Abbie stayed where she was and sent Klaus home. "I've asked the book to monitor Figghouse, and to let me know when the dog arrives. Figg has been with Nevin for centuries, Callum. He knows how to take care of himself with that fiend."

"He blinded Figg in one eye." Fists clenched, Callum paced the sitting room. "How can we stop him from doing that to Figg's last remaining eye or killing him?"

"He won't." Abbie shook her head, keeping her voice firm. "Nevin came to retrieve his most powerful weapon. The best protection we can give Figg is to convince Nevin we've let the dog go. If we don't, he might hurt Figg."

Callum sank back onto the loveseat and crossed his arms over his head. "What can we do then?"

"We will get him back."

"You can't promise that." His voice sounded dead, with not a note of hope to lighten it.

"I can promise to try." She took his hand. "I also know Figg. He's eluded his master before to visit me. Figg's a clever pup. He will probably find his way back to you before we've mounted our rescue."

Her phone buzzed. It was a text from Kiros, with a time and place to meet. Tonight. At St. Michael's.

Meeting the immortal on home ground suited her. She showed Callum the text before sending one to Talin.

*Change of plans. Explain later. My home. Half hour.*

She kissed Callum on his cheek and picked up her high heels. "Will you be all right?"

He nodded, eyes downcast.

"I'll text if I find anything more about Figg. Goodnight."

He caught her hand as she passed by him. "Sorry this date turned to dust."

Gazing into his upturned shell-shocked face, she leaned in and whispered in his ear the words she'd rehearsed all night. "I love you, Callum."

She drew back in time to see his gaze widen, and for one brief breath, his grief faded as a lightness eclipsed it. Then his pain returned, eclipsing every other emotion.

Outside Callum's home, she sat in her car and texted Yousef to cancel the S.O.S.

Before long, Judith flew across the night sky on Comet with her fiancé, Bran, Abbie's brother. The magical broom stopped beside Rosie.

Abbie gave them a quick rundown of what had taken place. "Will you two stay with Callum until Talin can come to keep his uncle company?"

Her brother gave her a thumbs up.

Waving goodbye, Abbie headed home. Callum was in excellent hands. Time to confront Kiros about his lies.

* * *

Abbie returned to her cottage and changed into jeans, a white tee, and a black leather jacket. She exchanged her fancy heels for her favorite sturdy black boots.

On her way downstairs, the doorbell rang. She sprinted to answer that call and to get on with her night errand.

At the door, Talin gave her a once-over, and then nodded, as if he approved. He, too, had dressed for battle in jeans, a checked shirt, a jacket, and steel-toed boots.

"Kiros should be here right about now." Abbie shut and locked her front door. "Arthur, shields up over both myself and Talin, please." No unnecessary risks tonight.

Her ring buzzed her finger in acknowledgment.

"Thanks." Talin studied the still night as they strolled to the car park. "Frees me to attend to other matters. What was the S.O.S. about? I was in class. I got out as quickly as I could and was on my way over when you sent your second text."

"Nevin swung by to retrieve Figg."

"What!" Talin stopped short, swinging back to her.

"He threatened to kill Callum, so Figg took himself to Nevin's car."

"Blimey. Is Uncle Cal alright?"

"He's in shock and grieving. Judith and Bran are with him until you can get there. I was a little worried that, if left alone, he might go looking for Figg." He had Levi to guide him now.

Talin took a deep breath and then nodded. "I'll move in with him later tonight. Unless you plan to?"

She shook her head. "Until Nevin's dealt with, I want to keep a closer eye on the kids."

He gave a grave nod, and they continued toward the church in weighted silence.

Light flared within the church, shining out through its three front windows to light up the car park.

Abbie and Talin glanced at each other and then they were up the church's front steps. She unlocked the front door and stepped inside, hurrying into the nave. All was quiet and dark. No light show in here now.

"What do you suppose that was?" Abbie ran her hand over the side wall, searching for the light switch.

"That was from us our arriving for this meeting." The quiet male voice came from the darkness of the church's chancel.

Kiros.

Light flared beneath the nave's ceiling. Abbie blinked to adjust to the brightness and took in Talin's raised hand that had made that miracle possible.

Ahead, Earth's immortal companion stepped forward, a tall, striking, dark-skinned man, dressed in a suit that boasted meticulously lined-up patterns and a perfect fit.

Abbie's hand found the light switch, and she turned on the overhead lights, adding to the glare. The overhead LED lights spread to the far corners of the church, showing a second visitor in the chancel.

Talin lowered his arm, extinguishing his magical light.

Behind Kiros, Pyramus strode up. He, too, was dressed in a suit, but his jacket was so standard in design that he could have purchased it off any clothing store rack. The Underworld immortal companion's large curled white horns glinted, striking against his deep red skin tone.

He flashed Abbie a twisted smile before his hooded gaze

took in Talin. "You brought a friend, too."

Wariness crept up her back at these two immortals being inside her church. Made sense, though. Unlike her cottage, this building wasn't protected against intruders. She'd merely locked it, which was too flimsy a protection to stop such powerful beings from entering.

During her Grimm adventures, Robert always reminded her to bring along one of her artifacts. Holding her left hand behind her back, she called on Kenny again. He settled within her palm and she put on the glasses. The artifact instantly shaded the entire rectangular church in shades of pink.

The church was mostly bare, with a few chairs stacked against one wall of the rectangular hall. Along one wall, lockers held first aid equipment.

She searched the entire interior for magical anomalies. There! Past the rood beam, in the chancel. Along the left wall, an archway slowly faded away.

That's how they had entered. Good to know.

"I don't recognize that artifact, Miss Grimshaw." Pyramus pointed to her specs. "What does it do?"

This demon had once refused to return three of her stolen artifacts that he'd found. Fear he'd take Kenny spread like a river of shivers. She shook off the sensation. Even if he did, she could retrieve her specs. To be on the safe side, though, she sent Kenny a silent order. *"Stay put."*

*"I will, Abbie."*

Pyramus's eyebrow rose, his eyes glinting. Of course, he was telepathic. He must have heard her and Kenny speak. "My specs are not relevant to our discussion tonight."

"Then let's crack on." Kiros pointed to the chairs and four

slid across the nave, floating a smidge above the floor. They positioned themselves to face each other, two by two, at a respectable distance apart.

These were chairs Abbie used for her students when she held first aid classes here. She'd purchased them from a school selling off surplus equipment. They had side arms with a small table hanging down one side. That side piece could swing up to hold books and pens. Hardly appropriate seating to offer two powerful immortals.

Kiros didn't seem to mind as he took his seat and stretched out his long legs, his face impassive. "What do you know about my son?"

"And what do you want from us?" Pyramus thumped onto his seat, his tail snapping out of the back opening of his wooden chair to flick back and forth.

Through Kenny's lenses, Pyramus exuded a crimson aura that swirled around him, whereas his brother seemed to be surrounded by a grimy blue haze with dark swirls.

Abbie aimed her first volley at Pyramus. "Kiros convinced us you were the one who killed my London friends and planned to release demons into Earth. He is not your friend. So, why are you here?"

The demon companion spurted out a chuckle and kicked at his brother's crossed feet. "Nice deflection, bro."

"Didn't work." Kiros's words held no hint of humor or remorse.

His brother raised and dropped his arms. "I'm here because, for centuries, we have tried and failed to contain the one you seek. I want to hear how you plan to do so."

"And to find out how you discovered I had a son." Kiros sat

up, drawing in his feet.

"I saw a Roman medallion around a mage's neck in 1703." Abbie turned to Kiros, who had a similar makeup and features to his brother, *sans* the horns and red skin. "It had your face engraved on it."

"You can time travel?" Kiros sat forward. "How?"

"Let's dispense with the 'how' questions." Pyramus's tone was surly. "She has a surfeit of magical artifacts that only she controls. That's all we are ever likely to discover about how she does what she does."

"It's dangerous to change the past." Though his words warned, Kiros's tone was questioning, as if there was something in his past he might want to alter.

"Goddess Kali told Abbie that affecting the past can alter karma." Talin's soft gaze remained fixed on his friend.

Kiros flung up his arms and looked around the church. "How many gods do you know?"

Abbie ignored his derisive tone. Or was that envy at her being acquainted with two gods, to his knowledge? He likely wouldn't want to hear the count was three, if she included Hafgufa, who resided within her right arm.

Time to get to the core of this discussion, Nevin. "We believe your son is the current Earl of Ashford."

"That's where he hides!" Pyramus slapped his thigh. "How did you find him out? We've sought him for centuries."

Abbie shifted her focus to the demon. His red skin was smooth, no hot patches, and his eyes glowed as if with a keen interest. Nothing suggested he lied. "You didn't know?"

"He's an elusive snake," Pyramus mimicked the movements of that reptile with his right hand, "who has mastered the art of replica magic."

"Why are you and your son estranged?" Talin inched his chair forward, closer to Kiros.

The Earth immortal's mouth clamped shut.

Pyramus observed Talin with a brooding gaze that unnerved her. At least his eyes weren't glowing red–his tell of when he was furious. He then tapped his brother on his arm. "Magnus and Kiros were once close."

So, Nevin's real name was Magnus.

"When the boy was young, the two were inseparable." Pyramus's gaze softened as it rested on his brother.

Odd, seeing compassion on this scary-looking demon.

"My nephew hero-worshipped his father. He wanted to be like him." He punched Kiros's shoulder, giving his brother a twisted grin that revealed one of his fangs before that sharp tooth went back into hiding. "Or what Magnus thought his father was like. Powerful, immortal, supreme among humans. My nephew was an idiot."

Pyramus's gaze went hard. "Everything my brother has, he earned. As I did in my realm. As our siblings have done in theirs. Something Magnus never understood. The Almighty did not gift us our success. We aren't friends with gods."

He grunted and glanced at Kiros, raising a questioning eyebrow. "Magnus's curiosity about how you became so powerful could be why he spied on our discussion that day. He likely wanted to learn your secrets."

Kiros's lips thinned, but he didn't argue the point.

"What did he learn from your conversation?" Abbie used a casual tone, tailored not to alarm, but she had a bad feeling about this glimpse into their history.

"Little." Kiros's gaze became drenched in anguish. "I punished him for his disrespect."

His stark emotion left Abbie's throat tight and her pulse pounding. Did Kiros have as vile a temper as Magnus? "What was his punishment?"

"I canceled our father-son visit to the Spell Gate market." Kiros bit out the words. "He'd been looking forward to that trip for weeks, counting the days. I hoped that would teach Magnus there are consequences to actions. Good or bad."

Relief came in a cool wave, slowing Abbie's heartbeats. Kiros hadn't physically harmed the boy. Surely a canceled trip couldn't have been dire enough to cause a centuries-old rift between father and son? Could it?

Magnus had wreaked havoc on Robert's life for closing his underworld gate. She shivered. What had he done to Kiros in retaliation for being denied that highly anticipated trip?

"Instead of accepting his chastisement like a proper gentleman," Kiros swiped his hand in the air, "my son turned his fury on his mother. He blamed her for telling on him."

Kiros swallowed, his hands curled into dark white-knuckled fists on his lap. "Magnus bludgeoned his mother to death using a bust of me she'd gifted him."

Abbie shuddered. Such a small trigger for such a violent reaction. Her breath stuck in her chest, tightening like a vise as she waited to hear how this horror story had developed.

"She was my wife! His mother!" Kiros' fists smashed down on his chair arms.

Abbie jerked at the crashing noise, raising her arms to fend off the shattered wood that flew around the room. They bounced off her shield.

Talin sucked in his breath.

She was trembling, trying to take in this horror story. No wonder these two had failed to patch up their relationship after such a devastating betrayal.

"After Kiros tracked his son down to where he cowered," Pyramus brushed slivers of wood off his lap, "He dragged Magnus back home and locked him in a windowless cell, with servants feeding him kitchen scraps." No judgment in the demon's words, merely acceptance.

Abbie now understood where Kiros's distrust of humans stemmed, why he had no friends. A human had tragically betrayed him. His beloved son. At least he had a caring brother on his side.

"I couldn't stand to look at him anymore." Kiros's words were choked, with tears filling up his eyes. He had the same look of agony she'd witnessed on Robert's face when the ghost spoke of the death of his child.

Pyramus's hard gaze met Abbie's, and he tilted his head toward Talin.

At some point, Talin had brought his chair right up to Kiros's side. He gently took the immortal's hand. "That's a lot of pain for both you and your son to carry for so long."

Kiros did not seem to notice Talin's closer presence or hear his words.

Pyramus leaned forward, a glow within his curled fist, as if he was prepared to strike at Talin if Abbie didn't do something. Now!

# Chapter Sixteen

Abbie studied Talin sitting close to Kiros, holding the immortal's hand. This gesture had upset Pyramus. Was the demon worried Talin meant to harm his brother? If so, he was mistaken. Talin took his friendships to heart.

Despite all the Standard Bearers' suspicions about Kiros, and what she and Talin had learned since entering this church, Talin's affection for Kiros had not faltered. If anything, he was more concerned than ever about his friend's well-being.

Abbie crossed her arms in a clear signal to Pyramus that she had no plans to interfere with Talin. Whatever her friend planned for Kiros, it would be for his good. Still, she was left with a tight chest, stiff shoulders, and nerves on edge.

Pyramus's lip rose in a snarl at her inaction.

"Magnus may not wish to relinquish his bitterness, Kiros," Talin's voice was the barest of whispers, "but isn't it time you released your anguish?"

Ah. That's what he was up to. Talin's newest use of his electromagnetic talent was to release emotional pain. He must want to heal Kiros of his torment. A plan that Abbie approved. A healed Kiros would be easier to trust than a volatile immortal consumed with grief and vengeance.

Kiros snapped his head around, as if he'd suddenly noticed how close Talin sat. Rearing back in his chair, he snatched back his hand. "I witnessed what you did with Mama D'leau. Releasing her pain. That won't work with me. You forget, I'm not human. Or a fae. I'm a creature unlike any you've encountered."

Talin stayed where he was. "Let me try."

During the ensuing tense silence, Pyramus's cool gaze studied Talin, eyes narrowed and lips pursed. Then he huffed out a breath, flicking his hand to extinguish the flame he'd built in his grip. "What harm could it do? If he succeeds, you will be rid of the bitterness that binds you. If he fails, you will be no worse off. But if he harms you, he will die."

Kiros glared at his brother, but when Pyramus did not rescind that suggestion, with an enormous put-upon sigh, Kiros slapped his left hand onto Talin's. "This is a waste of time."

Abbie released her pent-up breath. If Talin was to do this, she'd better distract Kiros. The process would go more smoothly if Kiros didn't fight the effort the entire time. "How long did you keep Magnus in that cell?"

Kiros's clamped lips didn't budge, so Pyramus broke the silence. "After a week, I visited him. To check if he was ready to repent for his misdeed and beg my brother's forgiveness. He wasn't. Magnus had already escaped."

Yikes! "And you've been searching for him since?"

Pyramus nodded. "Unsuccessfully."

Abbie's attention stayed rooted on Kiros and Talin as energy sparked within their clasped hands. Kenny showed her how Talin drew threads of dark energy out of Kiros.

"Magnus opened a door to your realm in the 1800s." Though she spoke to Pyramus, she couldn't drag her gaze from Kiros and Talin. "Robert and his company of soldiers shut it."

Pyramus's brows knit as his gaze moved from his brother to Abbie. "That was Magnus's second attempt at opening such a gate. I stopped his first. Any lingering affection my nephew had for me ended that day."

This was news! Abbie swung her startled gaze to Pyramus. He was opposed to an influx of his demons swarming into Earth? "Why does Magnus want to open such a door?"

"He hopes to punish Kiros. Overrunning Earth with demons would hurt his father's people. That would be a blemish on Kiros's watch."

"My son knows how to hold a grudge." Kiros's mutter was aimed at his chest, his chin tucked in. He was doing his best to ignore Talin's close presence.

"Why have you never stopped him?" She meant why hadn't he ended Magnus? Could he not bring himself to kill his son? He'd deflected Abbie from finding out about Magnus by throwing Pyramus in her path.

"My son is a human." Kiros shrugged, as if that were enough.

It wasn't.

At her raised eyebrow at Pyramus, the demon smirked, snorting smoke out of his nostrils. "Human lives end in the blink of an eye. We hoped we could wait him out and he would die a natural death."

"But he cast a spell to prolong his life." Abbie nodded, seeing their dilemma.

"His magical talent comes from his mother's lineage." Pyramus glanced at his brother. "Once rumor reached us about what he'd done, we were working on alternate solutions, but by then Magnus went into deep hiding."

This didn't sound as if these two immortals were in league with Magnus. Abbie's Grimm instincts hummed in agreement, opening the door to her sharing more information. "Two

Grimms wounded Magnus in 1703. Ever since, he's been aging and his powers have diminished."

Both brothers sat up.

Abbie met and held first Pyramus's, and then Kiros's gaze. "We believe your son's plan to open his next underworld gate might be prompted by more than revenge against his father. He is also desperate to preserve his life and may hope to use demon magic to do it. Whatever his motive, we can't allow him to open another such gate. We won't."

"How could you possibly know my son's intentions?" Kiros's face and body sank in, as if the air within him deflated at Abbie's suggestion she might kill to stop his son.

A part of him must still care about Magnus, the boy he'd once been so close to. The son he'd planned to take to the Spell Gate market, no doubt to show him off.

Abbie warmed to Kiros for that reaction, for it showed he could still love.

"Magnus once stole a child's puppy." Abbie girded herself before she continued, wondering if she were about to strike another of Kiros's hot buttons. "When the boy begged for his pet back, Magnus slew the child and his mother."

Kiros swallowed, his dark face turning paler.

She held her breath.

No eruption.

She breathed a sigh. Talin's efforts must be working. "Magnus cast a similar *live-long* spell on this pup, whom he named Figg, and changed the dog into a killing beast. Recently, I befriended Figg, and he showed me Magnus's intentions."

"Of course you did." Pyramus's sarcasm shot across the space between them.

Abbie ignored the demon's outburst. "Your son, Kiros, abandoned the pup two years ago. Talin's uncle, DCI Callum Radford, adopted that dog."

Kiros's attention swung to Talin. "Why would you allow your uncle to keep such a dangerous pet?"

"Uncle Cal's bonded with Figg." Talin spoke absently, his focus trained on his work. "They love each other."

"Best if he destroys that murderous mutt." Pyramus's tone was unsympathetic.

"Tonight," Abbie ground out the words, still riled about that loss, "Magnus retrieved the pup. No doubt because, when he opens his next underworld gate, until and unless he gains full control of the demons, Figg's his best defense."

Talin released Kiros. The immortal shook his freed hand, rubbing it. "Told you it wouldn't work."

Without responding, Talin carried his chair back to Abbie's side before slumping into his seat. He gave her a nod, appearing ashen, his fingers trembling.

In his seat, Kiros's shoulders were no longer hunched, nor were his fists clenched. His face was more relaxed, the lines on his forehead having smoothed out. Under Kenny's shading, the immortal's energy was also no longer streaked with darkness, but a brilliant clear blue.

Pyramus was staring at his brother, as if he couldn't believe what his eyes showed him. What did his demon gaze reveal about Kiros? Whatever it was, it must have shown him that the change in his brother was favorable.

She gave Talin's hand a congratulatory squeeze, and he flashed her a smug grin.

"Now we know Magnus's current disguise," Pyramus spoke

with confidence, "we will keep an eye out for his next move. If he opens another gate, I'll shut it."

Abbie shook her head. "Not good enough, because demons will have invaded our world by then."

Pyramus's mouth curved into a thin line of disdain. "No doubt that's as distasteful to you as it was for me to have a dangerous human mage dropped into my realm, uninvited."

At his sharp look her way, a wave of guilt warmed Abbie's cheeks. Using Kenny, she'd once disposed of an evil mage in Pyramus's underworld. Without asking his permission. Tonight, she'd even contemplated shoving Nevin in there.

Breaking eye contact with Pyramus, she pushed her specs up the bridge of her nose with a finger. Guess that last was no longer an option for the future. Pity.

At least, that decision would please Callum.

"What do you propose?" Kiros's gaze flicked between his brother and Abbie, as if mystified by their exchange.

"I'm traveling to Spain to check on the 1800s gate. If there's any sign your son wants to re-open it, we can set a trap."

"What do you need from us?" Kiros crossed his arms.

If she wished for his help, she'd better make her request now. After distrusting Kiros and his immortal siblings for years, she found that was no longer the case. Tonight's discussion cemented her new belief that Nevin, nee Magnus, was the real villain she must face.

As for these powerful immortals, Talin had blunted Kiros's simmering fury, making him more trustworthy. And she hated to admit it, but she was growing rather fond of Pyramus. He'd fed Jimi when he found him and kept the boy safe. He also cared deeply about, and was loyal to, his brother. All admirable attributes.

Their water brother had also helped her retrieve a sunken ship to help Mama D'leau. As for their formidable fae sister, she was at death's door. Considering all that, Abbie...

A hand settled over her shoulder, and she started, glancing back. An angel, *her* guardian angel, stood there, her gaze wide and lips pressed thin, as she studied the two immortals.

Under Kenny's shading, the angel appeared as a heavenly apparition, full of colors instead of her usual blinding white. Her wings were tucked and her gown was effervescent. Abbie's chest bloomed with hope. Was she here to help?

*"Be brave."*

Pyramus jumped up. He hurried over to Abbie, circling her. "Who said that? Who else is in here?"

Abbie stared at the demon, and when she glanced back, the angel was gone. She sighed, as deflated as Kiros had appeared earlier.

Pyramus's brows narrowed, his eyes squinting.

She let him stay mystified and sat back, focusing on Kiros. Brave, she would be. "You asked once if I would make a pact with you and your sibs. One in which, if we didn't harm any of you, all of you would leave us be. I am ready to make that pact, with one stipulation."

* * *

After their meeting, Abbie escorted Kiros and Pyramus out of the church. Once she shut and locked the church and turned back, the immortals were gone. Light flared from inside the church. Then the lights extinguished.

"Guess they left the way they entered St. Michael's." Abbie hugged Talin. "I'm glad you helped Kiros. Since he'll live forever, it's good he won't have to do it carrying that terrible burden."

He nodded, and releasing her, rushed toward his car with a backward wave. "I'm off to collect some clothes before heading over to Uncle Cal's."

"Give Callum my love."

Talin stopped in his tracks and swung back, surprise and delight shining in his gaze. "Truly?"

Abbie nodded, a smile tilting her lips up.

Once he'd driven off, Abbie headed toward her cottage. She made a mental note to check the left wall by the altar later. Tomorrow. Then she'd add some wards around the church to prevent anyone else from entering without her knowledge.

At her front door, she hesitated. Without Robert and the kids here, watching telly didn't appeal, and neither did reading a book. So, Abbie headed to her favorite place, the graveyard behind St. Michael's.

She strolled among the graves under the moonlight. Her life had become so busy that she'd forgotten how much she enjoyed this activity. Chatting with those who resided within these graves. As a child, she'd memorized all their names.

She swiped a tall gravestone. "Hello, Violet."

She went straight toward the secluded and forgotten section of this graveyard where Robert's grave had once rested until she moved him to lie beside his wife and child.

This grove was now a flower garden, with a bench where she could sit and read. She parked herself there and breathed deeply of the scented flowers.

"Did you have a fruitful visit with DCI Radford?" Robert was beside her on the bench.

She glanced at him and then swung to study the eastern horizon. The sky was filled with dawn's light. She must have been here for hours. The grove had performed its usual magic. She was at peace. "Nevin showed up demanding Figg back."

"Why did you not call me?"

"There wasn't much anyone could have done. When Nevin threatened Callum, Figg left with him. Then I received a message from Kiros that he was ready for our meeting. I met him in St. Michael's church tonight."

"With Talin?"

"Yes."

"How did that go?"

"I remembered your advice about taking an artifact during missions and called on Kenny." She patted her breast pocket. "He was quite useful." Then she shared what she'd learned from the two immortal brothers.

"Intriguing." He leaned back on the bench, stretching out his legs.

"The angel also showed up. I think because I was considering making a deal with the immortals."

"You made it anyway."

Abbie chuckled. "I believe this time, she approved of my plan. She told me to be brave. And yes, I did make that pact, with one condition. If we need help dealing with Magnus, they've agreed to assist."

"Do you believe they will?"

Abbie shrugged. "They accepted the pact."

"One thing I have learned from our association, Miss

Grimshaw," Robert flashed her a crooked smile, "is that you are resourceful when faced with danger. I have the utmost confidence in your ability to see this next stage through."

Abbie was about to suggest they head indoors when she sensed a subtle change in her immediate surroundings. She took out Kenny and put on the specs.

Directly ahead stood three ethereal beings. One woman and two children.

Pauline, Lizzy, and Claire.

Abbie's heart thundered at seeing them. About to jump up and run to greet them, she realized why they were here, and grabbed Robert's hand instead. It couldn't be time already? She hadn't defeated Magnus yet.

"What troubles you, Miss Grimshaw?"

"You have visitors, my lord." She smiled through her tears, overwhelmed by the ache of imminently losing him.

Robert glanced around, frowning.

She knew exactly when her guests became visible to Robert. The most joyous look came over his face. He couldn't take his eyes off Pauline. Then he noticed his Lizzy.

Robert stumbled to his feet.

Her hand slipped from his hold, unnoticed. Abbie rose, searching for a tissue in her pocket.

Robert knelt to hug his little girl and Abbie blew her nose and wiped her eyes.

Pauline touched his head, her gaze filled with longing.

Claire came over and took Abbie's hand. "Thank you, Godfairy Abbie."

"Hello, Claire." Abbie hugged the child, holding her tight. "I've been reading about your and Ruby's adventures to my kids. Why do you still look like a little girl when I know you grew up to live a full life?"

"Because this is how you remember me." Claire stepped back and twirled. "When we visit people, they always see us as they remember us best." She pointed to Pauline and Lizzy. "They came to see him, so I tagged along to thank you for saving me and giving me the very best life."

"You're welcome. Have you seen your parents?"

She nodded, smiling widely. "That's who I'm with and my husband, kids, and grandkids, and one day, you'll join us."

"I can hardly wait."

When she glanced over, Robert was kissing Pauline, who then drew back and whispered to him.

He turned to Abbie with a royal frown. "You asked her to come for me?"

"Don't be cross." Abbie went over and took his hand. "You taught me to be the strong woman I am today. Your job here is done. It's time to reunite with your family."

"But your greatest challenge is yet to come, Miss Grimshaw. And if I leave, the Standard Bearers will not be the blessed seven."

"We will manage. Trust that we will be fine."

Pauline whispered to him again.

He listened, frowning, and then his face cleared and he nodded. "My wife assures me you will not remain six for long." His eyes misted. "Thank you, Miss Grimshaw."

Abbie's throat was too choked up to utter a word. So, she simply hugged him.

He held her as tight. "Give my love to the children? And to Yousef, Talin, and Judith."

"I will." One moment she stood holding Robert and the next she was alone in the flowering grove. "Goodbye, Robert."

Abbie stood in that spot, unable to leave it, as if doing so was an admittance that he'd left her. Even though she'd been dreaming for years about Robert being back with his wife and child, of seeing that joy in his eyes, now the time was here, she was bereft.

The sun peeked over the horizon, brightening the morning light. In the distance, a drumbeat sounded. The grove grew lusher and more colorful as flowers bloomed to profusion, infusing the air with their lovely perfumes. From the entryway to this secluded area, Kali twirled into view to the sounds of that rhythmic drumming, her arms swaying in a beautiful dance.

Abbie couldn't help herself. She swayed in synch to the music and mimicked Kali's movements. She wasn't sure when, but at some point, her sorrow faded into the background and joy rolled in. When the drumming finally died down, they both sank onto the bench. Abbie was out of breath, while her whole being vibrated with bliss.

"*Namaste.*" Kali took Abbie's right hand, brushing the back of her fingers. Wherever the goddess touched, a pattern formed. Little dots and dashes that became lines and swirls.

"*You have done well.*" Hafgufa translated Kali's Hindi, including a hum of her own, which Abbie took as the normally taciturn water goddess's agreement with that assessment.

Abbie's cheeks heated, her delight soaring to the heavens at that joint approval from these two powerful beings.

"*The cover has been ripped off your enemy to expose the Jaan var.*" Kali moved on to decorate Abbie's other hand. "*But be wary, my versatile little Grimm Guardian. He now feels cornered. That makes him more dangerous than ever."*

"We don't yet know how to deal with him yet." Abbie's doubts crept in, landing her abruptly back on earth. "And we've now lost Robert."

*"You have all the tools you need for this mission. I have faith in your ability to see this last adventure to the end. Simply do as your angel advised."*

At the Indian goddess's departure, Abbie sat too wearied to move. Or did this lack of verve stem from Robert's absence?

Then an idea bloomed. She jumped to her feet, tiredness forgotten, and rushed home. Up in her room, she pulled up her laptop and typed out her next podcast.

She spoke about her adventures in the 1800s. With each word she typed, her tension and sorrows eased, as if sharing those stories lessened the weight she carried at saying goodbye to her gran and Claire, and helped her relive the joy and awe of that amazing journey.

The one topic she didn't mention was losing Robert. That was too raw. She wasn't ready to share that pain yet. Instead, she ended with her plans for the future.

*I'm about to set off on my most dangerous quest yet. And with this journey comes uncertainty.*

She paused a moment to reflect on her final words.

*Until next time, be kind to each other. Help each other. And be brave.*

THE END

* * *

Crave more of the Standard Bearers' adventures? In Book 8, **Death is Unleashed**[1], the final book in this extraordinary magical series, Abbie sets out to stop the villain who has been after her all this while. Her action incites the villain into rushing to complete his underworld revolution.

* * *

If you enjoyed this story, please consider leaving a brief review for this book wherever you purchased it. The review will help other readers decide if they'd enjoy reading it, too.

* * *

Sign up for Shereen's Newsletter to learn about her new releases.

http://www.subscribepage.com/c9u7e6

*Thank you for reading!*

---

1. https://books2read.com/DIDBook7

# Don't miss out!

Visit the website below and you can sign up to receive emails whenever Shereen Vedam publishes a new book. There's no charge and no obligation.

https://books2read.com/r/B-A-POZG-BVQJC

**BOOKS 2 READ**

Connecting independent readers to independent writers.

Did you love *Death is Delayed*? Then you should read *Death is Unleashed*[2] by Shereen Vedam!

**An old tragedy. A new mystery. A door to hell.**

A bus bombing killed EMT Abbie Grimshaw's team three years ago.

She's close to finding the culprit.

But he's also close to finding a way to destroy her, and he has much bigger plans.

He wants to open the gates of hell and unleash demons upon the Earth

Abbie and her Standard Bearers must stop the apocalypse

---

2. https://books2read.com/u/booNp1

3. https://books2read.com/u/booNp1

or will they be the first victims?

*If you enjoy thrilling mysteries with a fairy tale flavor, you'll love discovering this new face on the Grimm scene.*

**Pick up this magical adventurous mystery today**

Read more at www.shereenvedam.com.

# Also by Shereen Vedam

**Harrington Bay Mystery**
Sage It Out
Missing You


**Outside the Circle Mystery**
To Capture Love
Death Takes a Detour
Death Shifts Gears
Death Smells Disaster
Death Swipes Right
Death Comes Up Short
Death is Uncovered
Death is Delayed
Death is Unleashed


**Outside the Circle Mystery Boxed Sets and Bundles**
Outside the Circle Mystery: Boxed Set Books 1-3

**Tales of Ryca**
Hidden
Hushed


**The Cauldron Effect**
Coven at Callington
Warlock from Wales
Love Spell in London


**Standalone**
Tales of Ryca: The Complete Series
Torn
The Cauldron Effect: The Complete Series
Believe
Innocent


Watch for more at www.shereenvedam.com.

# About the Author

Once upon a time, USA Today bestselling author Shereen Vedam read fantasy and romance novels to entertain herself. Now she writes heartwarming tales braided with threads of magic and love and mystery elements woven in for good measure.

Shereen's a fan of resourceful women, intriguing men, and happily-ever-after endings. If her stories whisk you away to a different realm for a few hours, then Shereen will have achieved one of her life goals.

*Please consider leaving a review wherever you purchased this book.*

Read more at www.shereenvedam.com.